AFFLUENZA

Published by Offense Mechanisms, an imprint of Silverthought Press
www.offensemechanisms.com
www.silverthought.com

Cover photograph by Mark R. Brand
Cover design by Paul Hughes

ISBN: 978-0-9841738-0-8

AFFLUENZA
BY DAVID LABOUNTY

OFFENSE MECHANISMS
PHILADELPHIA / NEW YORK

Maybe you like yourself.

Maybe you don't.

Maybe you're asking yourself that very question right now as my words jar your curiosity.

But don't answer. Not now. Wait.

Maybe you're one of the virtuous types without an ill thought in your head. Maybe your thoughts are free of lust and violence and full of nothing but happy and pleasant things. Maybe you're one of the virtuous types and you pay your bills on time no matter what. You pay your bills because it kills you to be late, to be behind, to be in debt too long.

It kills you to be irresponsible.

And I have to tell you, irresponsibility does kill.

Maybe you're one of those indifferent types. Maybe you don't give a shit what anybody thinks about you. Maybe you don't care if you piss the world off or if you fall behind on bills and payments and maybe you don't care if you're working or not. You know everything will fall into place. You know that you'll be taken care of. You know that you won't starve and you know that you won't have to live on the street and you don't care about a lot of things, things like the grass that grows knee-high in June before you decide to cut it, and maybe you don't care if your kids are doing well in school and making friends and learning how to be responsible young citizens. You hate responsibility. It kills you to be responsible.

And I have to tell you, responsibility does kill.

But I don't want you to think about yourself right now. This is about me, and maybe after you understand me then you will be better able to judge yourself.

I am reminded of a line from a song I heard about a million times in college, usually with a joint or a beer in my hand. It wasn't a song I particularly liked because it was stoner music and even though I puffed I was never really a stoner but smoking weed was a requirement in my fraternity of suburban white boys stuck going to college in Bumfuck, Michigan.

All you create. All you destroy.

What have you created? A home of some sort, even if you're thirty-five years old and that home is a bedroom in your mother's house. Your bedroom, your space, is still a home. Maybe you've created a career. You may consider yourself successful, working for some firm or corporation and moving up some sort of managerial or executive ladder. Maybe you've made a career of manual labor, ditch digging, car washing, office cleaning. No matter what it is, you've created something, a track of something definable. Maybe you've created a family, a spouse and kids that wouldn't exist without you. Maybe you've created a family and it may exist in spite of you. Maybe you've created love. Maybe you've created hate. I don't know.

Everybody's different.

What have you destroyed? I don't care how virtuous and pure you are, you've destroyed something. Friendships that drift apart, thoughts and memories you don't want to keep. Maybe you've destroyed your pride or your identity in an attempt to keep all of the things you've created, things like your family or your career. Maybe you've destroyed the things you love and tried to rid yourself of the things you hate. I don't know.

Everybody's different.

And that's all life is, really: a cycle of birth and death, of sorrow and joy.

A cycle of creation.

A cycle of destruction.

I know a little bit about creation.

But I know a lot more about destruction and there is a point in my life that I destroyed everything and let me tell you a little bit about my life, my life after the destruction:

I thought I would keep things normal for a while and probably forever.

I thought I would keep the dishes clean and the bed made and the rug vacuumed.

But no.

The contractors fixed up the house and it felt new again. I thought I would have some pride in the newness, a fresh start. A clean slate.

Yes and no.

The dishes are piled in the sink and they spill onto the counter and I rinse them as I need them.

I see no point in washing anything and I don't want to pump you full of psychobabble but I don't see the need for cleanliness.

I am more than dirty on the inside.

I never make the bed nor do I wash the sheets and they are stained with my sweat and other fluids that I don't need to mention.

And the carpet. Well, it's probably supporting an ecosystem of its own by now.

I can't keep things normal because I didn't realize how indifferent I would be.

Maybe not indifferent; I still fight the war and there is a burning in my groin that just doesn't go away but I feel emotionally dead on the inside and I try to look in the mirror to find clues. I love looking in the mirror. My eyes used to twinkle and shine. Now they look the same but they're empty.

Picture putting in a blank videotape and hitting play.

I thought a burden would have been lifted after the destruction and I thought I would have felt vindicated. I thought I would have felt just. But I misjudged myself; I misjudged the amount of love I actually created for others. I misjudged the amount of love I destroyed inside of me.

But you know how it is. You know that the stress of living can bury all kinds of things.

Stress can bury love.

Responsibility can kill it.

And I've learned, through all of this sadness and domestic disorder, just how sad I am. I would kill myself if I wasn't so selfish and afraid.

I created this for me, to ease my stress, to kill my responsibilities.

But stress doesn't end.

If you were to look at the outside of my house you would think it looks normal enough. It looks like every other house in the neighborhood. It is a two-story Colonial with an attached garage and the roof and gutters are still intact and I can afford to pay someone to cut and edge the grass and trim the bushes. It is a typical house in a typical suburb choked with typical houses and typical people.

And that's part of the problem, so many people trying to be the same.

And if you were to look at me, at least from the back or on my good side, you would think I look normal enough. White male, fortyish, average height, averagely overweight and driving a newer automobile just like every other fortyish male in every other typical suburb.

And it's not like I've imploded completely. I still go to work every day where I sit at a desk and deny claims in order to make my six figures a year and that may sound like a lot of money to some people. It may sound like a lot of money to most people.

But enough is never enough.

I used the days that followed the destruction to my full advantage. I used them to miss work and I felt guilty about being so glad to not have to go to work.

"I won't be coming to work today. My wife and kids just got killed," and that's all I said to my boss, who already knew what happened but pressed me for details and piled on sympathy.

I gave him the details and I took his sympathy as if I really needed his sympathy and I cried into the phone like a grieving husband and father should and I was so glad that I didn't have to go to work.

It was like the death of my wife and children was worth it, worth the reward of sleeping in for three weeks. The death was worth the reward of drinking beer all day and every day and eating pizza and I did all the things I wanted to do, after my three-week-long hospital stay. I watched rented pornos until four in the morning and woke up at two in the afternoon and went back for more beer and more movies as if I was trying to catch up on my gluttony and lust and sloth.

But don't judge me, not yet. Each person deals with grief in his or her own way and my way was to not grieve at all. I guarantee there are men out there, recently widowed, who went out and bought a new set of golf clubs or a sports car while their dead wife's body was still warm.

There was the funeral and I missed the funeral.

But I saw part of it on the local TV news while lying immobile in my hospital bed and there were a couple of cousins watching it with me and I cried and looked forlorn and pious. But that was for the cousins.

I was far from pious away from other people's eyes, back home behind closed curtains and blinds, at home with a clutter of beer cans and pizza boxes across the kitchen and living room. I was fine watching young girls squirm and moan on my television screen while the still slightly charred remains of my kids' rooms remained undisturbed, their bookcases full of barely singed books and toys, the still intact stuffed animals on their beds waiting for them to someday come home.

And the stuffed animals are waiting still.

I felt something like grief later and I feel it now. Grief without sorrow. Grief without melancholy. Grief that just is. I feel it as I try to live like everybody else, as I try to feel like just-another-face behind the wheel during that morning commute.

But no one has my face. No one has the thoughts that go with my face.

And memories. You wouldn't want my memories. I could kill myself over my memories.

But I'm too selfish and *waaay* too lazy to kill myself. So instead I come home from work every night, make myself a rum and Coke or a Jack and Coke and I watch the network news and I microwave a dinner and throw the empty carton on the kitchen counter or table and there it stays until the arrival of too many ants dictates that it's time to take out the trash.

I watch more news and then maybe a ball game that I really don't care about and then I get ready for bed. I brush my teeth and put on a stained t-shirt and stained boxer shorts and I stare at my face in the mirror for a long while. Try that sometime. You'll be surprised how often your face changes as shadows fall and as your eyes move in and out of focus. My face will change a hundred times during my nightly half-hour stare-down.

I think it's because I'm a hundred different people and if I am that means you are too.

I guess it just depends how different those hundred people are.

I'm going to tell you a little bit about the beginning even though the beginning has nothing to do with what happened later.

I am going to tell you about creation. I created a lot of things early on.

The destruction came later and don't worry, there will be a lot of destruction later.

An uncomfortable amount of destruction.

Let's go back twenty-five years or so. Let's go back to 1983 and I was right out of college and I was thinner and I had more hair.

A lot thinner. A lot more hair.

I was right out of college armed with a business degree from one of the state colleges in the northern Lower Peninsula, about four hours away from my hometown suburb of Detroit and you probably already know there is precious little that is homey about a suburb.

If you've been to Ann Arbor, Michigan then you've been to Evanston, Illinois and if you've been to West Allis, Wisconsin then you've been to Glen Burnie, Maryland and so it goes.

Or, to make it clearer, if you've been to a Starbucks in Kirkland, Washington then you've been to a Starbucks in Cambridge, Massachusetts. Different but not different.

I couldn't afford to go out of state for school even though I wanted to. No one offered me scholarships or anything so I had to go where my college fund could send me, and that was to a small town full of poor and overweight people who hated college students even though they forged their meager existence out of them. Think landlords and bartenders. Think campus security guards and fast-food drive-thru workers.

And I did well enough in college, socially and academically. I joined a fraternity and my brothers and I have since drifted apart even though most of them live around here somewhere but we're nothing more than drops of water in a giant sea of monotony. I went to most of my classes and studied and drank a lot of beer. I got laid a few times and I graduated without distinction and got my degree and then it was a job for the same insurance company I work for now.

They hired me in at $19,000 a year.

I felt rich.

My old man said, "Attaboy. It's a start. A damn good start. Play your cards right and you'll be just like me." And I was all right with that but I wanted a hotter wife than my mother.

Not that I judge my mother on some sexual scale, but you know what I mean.

I bought a car. A white Ford Mustang. I bought new clothes. Oxford shirts with stripes and thin fluorescent ties. I bought polo shirts for after work and on weekends and I turned the collars up. I bought different kinds of hair gel and bottles upon bottles of cologne and aftershave. I bought cassettes and a stereo and a VCR and I rented a one-bedroom apartment along the same strip that my office is on. The office building was then new, in the shadow of a suburban mall, and it is made mostly out of glass and pyramid shaped with a sunny atrium that greets you as soon as you enter the revolving door.

I would learn to hate the sight of that atrium and I hate it still as I walk through it every day, past the plastic plants toward the elevator that carries me fourteen stories up to my office at the top of the pyramid.

I've seen a lot of people come and go through that atrium but I still remain. I prosper and thrive like a weed in an ignored garden.

I haven't destroyed my career. Not yet.

I was hired as a customer service rep and that's where I met Deidre, my future wife. She was hired right out of college, too, a different state college in a different small city and she also had a business degree.

They hired her in at $16,000 a year.

She felt rich but she was a little more practical back in those days and she moved in with her mom (the next suburb over from where I grew up) rather than get an apartment on her own and there she stayed until suave and thin and feathered hair me swept her off of her feet.

Or something like that but minus the romance.

We sat side by side in the phone bank and we would chit-chat during the idle moments that were allowed a representative for Midwestern Accident and Life and the chit-chat that went on for a few weeks led to flirting for a few more weeks and that led to going to lunch together every day for a few weeks and then after about four months we finally went out on a real date. I picked her up in my Mustang that was soaked in air freshener and I was soaked in cologne and hair gel to keep my thick and long hair close at the sides.

I wore a gold chain around my neck and I'm too embarrassed to tell you what I put in my cassette player when I picked her up but the singer was a man in drag.

I took her to a nicer restaurant near our office where all the Midwestern bigwigs went for lunch. A steak and lobster kind of place. The kind of place that used to exist in abundance before the chain restaurants took over the landscape.

You and I, we've both eaten at Chili's or Applebee's or maybe Ruby Tuesday or Friday's.

Maybe you're like me and you've eaten at all four. A lot.

Anyway, I took her to dinner and then a movie and back to my place and we screwed.

Just like that.

And then we got together once a week for a few months. Dinner and a movie and then we screwed unless there was a holiday or a menstrual situation or if she forgot to take her birth control pills and the pills—she kept them a secret from her mother.

Her mother didn't like me. This I could tell and Deidre confirmed this early on.

"There's something about you that rubs her the wrong way," Deidre told me as I opened the door of my Mustang for her on a summer night. I had made a reservation at a nice restaurant that really didn't require reservations.

That kind of stung me a little bit, not the not needing reservations but whatever it was about me that rubbed her mother the wrong way.

"I'm a good guy... I'm good to you," I told her in a whiny kind of voice to match my assaulted ego.

"I know that. I wouldn't date you if you weren't, but she says there's something about you." She buckled herself in and spoke without looking at me and come to think of it, we always spoke without looking at each other.

"What is there about me?"

"I don't know. She just says there's something wrong with you, something bad, but I don't know what she's talking about."

"Well, that's bullshit," I said and I fiercely gripped the leather steering wheel cover that I had installed earlier that week and my knuckles grew pale while my face turned red. I was angry and it wasn't because Deidre's mom didn't like me.

It was because even then I knew deep down there was something wrong, that I could do things that other people would find horrific even if I didn't quite know what those things were, or would be.

"Hey, don't get angry," Deidre said and she put her hand on my zipper and I felt my cock grow and she felt it too so she gave it a little squeeze. "My mom just wants me to be careful, that's all."

I backed out of the driveway and waved to Deidre's mother as she stood in the living room window glaring at me.

She didn't wave back.

And she never did wave, not ever, nor did she ever visit me at the end, after the destruction, even though everybody else who knew me did.

Everybody but my father and my mother-in-law.

Back to the beginning of the end of Deidre's life.

Deidre and I dated and went to lunch and fucked and went to dinner and fucked for about a year and after a year I was pretty much broke. I had missed a payment on my Mustang and was late on my rent a few times and that caused embarrassing phone calls while I was at work and I had to explain myself and get defensive in between my regular phone calls dealing with customers in an offensive sort of way.

"Sorry, Mr. Jones, but it's your fault you lost the use of your arm. Your policy clearly states no walking on your roof.

"It doesn't matter if you were cleaning your gutters or not. You're supposed to hire a professional to do that for you."

And so it went until the bank called or my landlord called and then my voice got really soft and I'd beg for forgiveness and extensions and I would get them.

But my dates with Deidre got cheaper and cheaper.

Instead of going out to eat it was McDonald's in my apartment and she offered to help pay for stuff and having Deidre offer to pay for stuff was something akin to castration. A real man doesn't need his woman to pay for stuff. A real man provides. A real man fucks his woman's brains out and leaves her begging for more.

A real man doesn't have his woman buy his quarter-pounders for him.

I had to give up cable TV and I felt like such a fool adjusting my rabbit ear antennas.

I started to struggle. I started to sweat a little between paydays. Money that had seemed endless when I first started working soon seemed like it could never possibly be enough and what cheap bastards my bosses were for paying me, a professional, the same salary as school teachers and policemen.

And they were cheap bastards, my bosses at Midwestern Accident and Life. They still are cheap bastards and they try to hang on to every penny and that has been my job for most of my career, telling people they're not getting any of our pennies, telling people they're screwed for life after a tornado tears the roof off of their house. I tell them they're screwed even when the roof lands on their minivan and totals it.

"I'm sorry, Mrs. Drinkwater, but you declined the tornadoes in the spring coverage. You would have been fine if this was a tornado in October…"

And yes, I sometimes have a hard time falling asleep at night.

Even monsters have pangs of conscience.

Even monsters have souls.

But sleep, it always comes eventually, sleep that is deep and still.

I struggled mightily with bills for six months and Deidre stuck with me. We were in love then and in lust; we couldn't get enough of each other.

And then we decided it was time to take things to the next step and it was the Eighties.

We moved in together.

We moved into a townhouse in Sterling Heights not very far from where we worked. We got a nice place, really out of our reach, even though we were both paying for it. My Mustang looked silly in the parking lot full of Volvos and Audis and BMWs and we felt like a part of the yuppie class.

There were no kids or old people in our row of townhouses.

My parents were fine with me living with Deidre.

You sound so perfect together, my mother said.

Deidre and Chuck.

Deidre and Chip.

Deidre and Chas.

And we had to furnish our new townhouse. Deidre had to dig into her savings for most of it because what was in my wallet was all I had to my name and her savings were blown in a hurry because we had to have the latest designer furniture, you know, sectional couches that took up half the living room and matching recliners with ottomans that took up the rest as well as a large screen TV that lorded over it all.

And then there was the king-sized waterbed and satin sheets because we were the sexy type and fucked all the time.

And then there was the microwave oven and coffeemaker and Deidre bought the most expensive kinds.

"I'll make it up to you," I said, as a way of thanking her for buying all the stuff. I was able to look past my machismo when it came to buying furniture. Buying furniture wasn't a dinner date; there was no code of chivalry that I knew of that said a woman couldn't buy all the household furnishings.

And I did make it up to her and then some, only to destroy it all in the end.

And it was a good life, good enough, playing house together and sleeping together and paying bills together.

Going broke together.

And Deidre became expensive. She learned how to keep her little ass and tits decorated. Nice hair that cost a bundle to cut, color, and style. Press-on nails applied by Asian women in those nail salons that started popping up all over the place. And clothes. Deidre liked her clothes and she bought dresses and skirts and tight jeans and nice shoes and I liked her to look good.

Right up to the end.

And I wasn't cheap to live with either. I figured a rising professional should enjoy the finer things in life. Good liquor, a good stereo, and I bought a shitload of cassettes in those days, cassettes that would be worthless three or four years later when CDs came pouring in.

So, we lived well but we lived hand to mouth. The money would go as soon as it came in and payday would arrive and we'd greet our paychecks like a junkie getting a fix, the cashed check like a euphoric shot in the arm.

But we couldn't control ourselves and we started to fight, bickering about who had to pay what percentage of the utility and phone bills or whose turn it was to buy groceries even though our groceries were nothing more than frozen dinners that could be zapped in the microwave and cold cereal.

The fighting started to become mortal after a few months of so many excesses. We stopped talking at work, which was fine because the upper management wasn't too keen on two co-workers cohabitating.

But then an idea came to my head, a glorious and wonderful idea, and I smacked myself in the head for not thinking of it sooner.

A credit card. I applied for and received a credit card with a thousand-dollar limit.

And then the party really got started.

The credit card was a Visa from a local bank that I had banked with all of my life, ever since my mother made me empty my piggy bank when I was nine and dragged me by the hand and made me open up my first savings account.

And that account, you know, it never had a lot of money in it.

I've always liked to spend it, even when I was a kid. There was candy and baseball cards in elementary and junior high and then there was fast food and records and cologne and gas for my parents' car in high school.

Anyway, I got the Visa and I felt powerful, twenty-four and affluent, and I didn't consider the payments or the interest at eighteen percent.

Eighteen was just a number.

Eighteen was just a number and I didn't give a shit about paying interest. I was broke but I felt on top of the world. I had a hot girlfriend that I could bang every night and this was a huge feat for a guy like me who was a sophomore in college before he ever really kissed a girl.

And I was a junior before I ever got laid.

So I got the credit card and it was a new stereo and I got it at the electronics store between my office building and the mall. I haggled with the salesman and I got two extra speakers thrown into the deal.

I wired our bedroom for sound so Deidre and I could do it to Huey Lewis or Duran Duran.

Deidre liked doing it to Cyndi Lauper. You know, girls just want to have fun.

I liked doing it to Prince when I wanted to be raunchy.

So there we were going broke after we got paid and fucking and watching rented movies in our new VCR and all of a sudden my credit card wasn't enough.

I maxed it out.

So Deidre got one too.

And then I got another one while making the minimum monthly payments on the one I already had and that was followed by an Amoco gas card because I never had the cash to put in my tank and gas was getting expensive, hovering around a buck twenty-five a gallon, and it was starting to hurt.

And it was around that time that I got a promotion. I did so well in dealing with unhappy customers, you know, pacifying them without satisfying them, that I got sent from the first floor up to the third floor and got a job in the claims analysis department.

And I got a raise.

Twenty-four and I was making twenty-two grand a year, had a hot girlfriend, had a cool place to live, and I felt like things were going my way.

But they weren't. They were starting to go the other way, but I was too addicted to clothes and cologne and sex to notice.

Now, you're probably thinking to yourself that Deidre and I couldn't last. You're probably thinking that a relationship based on sex and music and debt can't last long.

Well, you're wrong.

You're wrong because we both understood each other the way recovering alcoholics and drug addicts understand each other.

We were birds of a feather and if you scratched the skin of either of one of us you'd find we were both the same on the inside.

We were both nothing.

And let me tell you, there's no one happier than one who has nothing on the inside.

Think about it. If your life is full of meaning and concern then you are probably miserable and angry a lot of the time or maybe even scared. You know, in those days there was talk of nuclear war with the Russians and it was a tense time.

That is if you watched the news. And if you watched the news you might have been afraid of Colonel Qaddafi in Libya because he was terrorizing innocent women and children by hijacking boats and planes and killing any American on board.

I had absolutely no knowledge of terror. Terror was—and is—just a word.

We didn't watch the news. We watched sitcoms and rented movies and after a few years we started renting pornos.

Sometimes you have to take the nothing on the inside to the next level and Deidre and I were no different. We got sick of going out to eat and coming home and doing it to music even though we were still in love with each other and I was certainly in love with myself.

Because in 1987 I got another raise, up to twenty-six grand a year and I was given a secretary. Deidre was still in customer service, but she was making twenty grand a year and I could see our meteoric rise into privilege.

We talked about buying a house.

But that had to wait. We weren't ready to spend our money in a meaningful way. We wanted to keep on renting pornos and doing it after sitting on the couch a few minutes into the movie.

We were so dumb. We thought for the longest time there should be some sort of plot to a porno.

But anyway, we watched those plotless movies and had plotless sex, you know, different positions that we learned from the movies and we went on with our plotless lives and we really hadn't discussed our future together. We knew we had a beginning but we didn't foresee a middle with any sort of definition.

A middle with any sort of meaning.

And the pornos gave us new ways to spend money. It gave us new ways to swipe our plastic. There was lingerie for Deidre, who laughed the first time she saw herself in the mirror wearing a garter belt and stockings and she looked frightened the first time she saw herself in latex.

And then there were more satin sheets for our bed and a mirror on the ceiling and I am man enough to admit that I bought one of those rings to put around my cock to make it stay up even after I came.

Really.

I wanted to fuck and fuck even if I couldn't feel a thing.

And in between the sex there were trips to the restaurants with friends we met from work or with friends from our high school and college days that seemed so long ago even though they really weren't.

And none of our friends were as quite as empty as we were. We only managed to go out with other couples once or twice and then we never heard from them again.

Really.

The Eighties ended and it seemed that things changed with that transition. The world moved into the end of the Soviet Union and the birth of fax machines and the music we used to do it to was suddenly so very out-of-date.

That realization hit home when I saw a cassette from The Cars in the discount bin at Kmart. The music of my glory days was only $1.99.

And then Deidre and I started to change and you know that change, the way your body changes from late adolescent to young adult and all of a sudden you're thirty and you don't burn off the combo meal from McDonald's the way you used to.

My pants started getting tight. My thin and past-tense ties became ramped as they traveled toward my belt. Deidre had to go from a size 4 to a 6 and she was ready to commit suicide over it and the size change ended her lingerie modeling and fucking career.

She wanted to make love with all the lights off instead and even that became infrequent.

She wanted meaning.

She wanted our lives to follow some sort of plot, you know, like in all the normal movies. Boy meets girl and they fall in love and get married, make babies. All of that.

She was starting to feel mortal. Her vanity was tinged with her weight gain and the wrinkles forming around her eyes. She was no longer happy driving her Grand Am and going out every weekend to dinner and movies and shopping.

And me?

My vanity was tinged too. I had to buy new pants and shirts that were bigger in the neck and I bought wider ties and I felt sad about that. I was no longer the young man in the office, no longer so cool.

My Mustang was in and out of the shop and it started getting rust spots so I bought a Ford Probe instead and I thought I could swing it at three hundred bucks a month after trading in my Mustang.

And I guess I did swing it, but everything was a struggle. An unfulfilling struggle.

The Probe didn't give me the happiness the Mustang did. It was just a car even though I did my best to put my personality on it, you know, pine tree air fresheners hanging from the rear view mirror and I even put in a CD player and a moon roof. Nothing like the summer breeze ruffling your hair.

Even if your hair is disappearing.

And mine wasn't a gradual hair loss. I didn't lose it the way so many uncles and cousins did, you know, their hair just a little thinner with each passing holiday when some smartass cousin or uncle says to everyone that so-and-so has a testosterone problem and the hair is falling out because so-and-so is too much of a man. My hair came out in clumps and it became noticeable one morning after my shower. I was standing in front of the steamed up mirror and I was shaving with my new Gillette refillable razor that I bought because of the commercials on TV.

I was shaving and studying my suddenly fleshy face in the steamed-up mirror. I noticed my double chin, my blood-pressure-red cheeks and my forehead growing and shining like a searchlight suddenly naked where so much hair used to be.

And then I thought about my father for a moment, how he looked when he was my age, at the ripe old age of twenty-eight.

I was three when he was twenty-eight and he was almost completely bald and already overweight but he was a god to me and I embraced his girth and baldness because that's who and what he was and that's who he still was up until the end but he was stooped over by then and had to breathe with the aid of portable oxygen tanks.

Smoking will kill you.

Smoke will kill you.

Anyway, I remembered my father and I shuddered and finished shaving and I tried to drown my sorrow with a gallon of aftershave.

I was into Gillette aftershave then because it matched my razor.

But I wasn't ready to embrace anything other than a body that could fit into the same jeans I wore in high school. I wasn't ready to accept hair that wasn't so thick and full that it required ample amounts of mousse to hold in place.

So Deidre and I joined a gym and got a lifetime membership for something like three hundred bucks each.

They took our credit cards and swiped them.

We of course had to buy workout clothes and Deidre had to be accessorized. Her workout shoes had to match her spandex shorts and t-shirts and I had to have the best cross-training shoe the kid at the mall could sell me.

And if you saw me now you would know I didn't go the gym for life.

I bought Rogaine for my hair along with powders and pills that were designed to grow my hair back. None of it worked.

I'm now almost as bald as a hard-boiled egg and I've never really been affluent enough to go and get hair transplants.

But I've thought about it.

And it was at that point—that point when Deidre and I both felt touched by mortality—that this story begins.

Really begins.

There was a certain amount of pressure from our families after Deidre and I lived together for so many years without changing anything.

My parents wanted us to get married.

Deidre's mom wanted her to get married too, but to someone besides me.

And Deidre and I were happy with our aimless lives probably because we didn't know they were aimless until we realized we were starting to get old even though we were still young.

And Deidre decided she wanted to get married too, at about the same time the other guys in the phone bank stopped flirting with her in between calls.

I'm the fat old lady, she would tell me.

And I thought we should make a change too, I mean, I was balding and gaining weight and me in my Probe didn't turn heads at all.

And that hurt.

We were both hurt and we weren't doing anything about it.

We had both started going to the gym by this point.

We had both stopped going to the gym by this point.

So, I figured what the hell. Deidre and I, we made a good team. We understood each other and I was pretty sure I wanted to be a father someday and Deidre was the only one who seemed to like me for more than three months.

And three months is a stretch. I had zero girlfriends in high school and only a handful in college and none ever stuck with me for more than a couple of months.

Usually they left after we had sex a few times, now that I think about it.

And now that I think about it, I never broke up with any of them. I never dumped any of them.

I was the dumpee.

You know, I should look some of them up, those girls in college who blew me off, and see how they're doing. I mean, I'm single now. I've got money for Viagra and I keep a bottle of it on my nightstand but I haven't had a chance to use it in a truly spontaneous way (it's there just in case) and I have to wonder what these girls look like now.

I doubt they look as hideous as me.

But still, I'd like to swallow a couple of Viagra and really give it to 'em and I have to admit, the only way I get laid now is if I pay somebody and I don't know how good in the sack I ever was. Judging by my track record in college I must have sucked.

But Deidre had no complaints. At least none that she mentioned and I guess we had the same amount of carnal experience, you know, some sex in college but never a steady and torrid thing like we had with each other in our early days.

And then came our decline.

Our destruction.

And I guess we both got married to end some misery, to create something new, to maybe change us.

But people don't change.

And that's the problem.

I could flash forward through a lot of things, and I'm going to. I could fly past the wedding, my promotions, childbirth, Deidre's decision to quit going to work and become a housewife.

None of that really matters. None of that explains my face.

None of that explains the things I've created.

But it does explain the things I've destroyed.

Our wedding was a disaster, but not in the way you're thinking. No one ran away from the altar and no one got so drunk during the reception that they had to be hauled away on a stretcher though that would have made it interesting at least, somebody's fat old aunt or uncle puking on the dance floor, breaking limbs.

But no, our wedding contained no spectacles. A spectacle of any kind would have been better than what happened.

Our wedding was sad. So sad it was pathetic.

A shine came to Deidre's face during the early days of wedding planning. This had to have been in late 1991 and the goal was a spring wedding, Saturday, May 16, 1992.

She bought all of the bridal magazines and her mother helped her pick out a wedding gown and Deidre wanted a big wedding.

About 300 people, she said. 300 is a good number, you know, not too small but not too big and she compared us to Sean Penn and Madonna and I think they were already divorced by that time but I don't remember.

I do remember that I liked to do it to Madonna's music, once upon a time, before my gut got in the way, before I worried about the part in my hair coming undone and exposing my baldness.

So the plans proceeded and Deidre's mother helped her with everything. I thought that maybe she had taken a shine to me, you know, because she helped with the wedding.

She helped with everything except the finances.

"No, she doesn't like you," Deidre said. "She's accepting you. She's tolerating you. She's going to learn to live with you because you make me so happy."

And Deidre said that without smiling, without looking me in the eye.

So the wedding plans proceeded. A church was secured, the same Methodist church Deidre attended as a child. The minister didn't care that neither one of us had been inside a church in over a decade or more. He didn't care, he just made sure the day was clear on his calendar and he made sure he got paid half up front and the other half just before the I Do's.

And then there was the hall rental and it was some Italian banquet place in the city. It was owned by Russians and they recommended a caterer, some Serbian family that made Italian food and it was atrocious, but that wasn't the bad part.

I barely remember the food. I doubt anyone remembers the food from our wedding. There were other, more horrible things to remember.

Deidre found her gown; it was some white thing she bought at a boutique in the mall near our office. I forget how much it cost.

Deidre paid for it with a credit card, the first credit card that had both of our names on it, and she bought it a little on the small side. She wanted to lose weight for the wedding.

"Sex—we'll have more sex," she said. "It burns calories." And I still remember how she looked in that wedding dress, the flesh of her arms and stomachs pinched into rolls and folds.

A tuxedo style was decided on for me and my best man and the groomsmen, as well as dresses for the bridesmaids as well as what sort of flowers to put on the altar and as centerpieces at the tables during the reception.

And that's when the tragedy started to unfold.

It was tragic because Deidre and I really didn't have any friends.

I convinced my older brother to be my best man and my mother convinced second and third cousins to be my two groomsmen as well as ushers.

Deidre didn't have it so easy.

There was her sister but her sister wasn't talking to her because her mother poisoned her mind about us, about how evil and opportunistic and immoral I was and I didn't think so at the time. But again, I knew there was something wrong but I thought

I was basically a good guy. I viewed myself the same way you view yourself.

Decent but flawed.

So Deidre had a hard time recruiting bridesmaids, not to mention a maid of honor.

Ultimately one of my cousins was her maid of honor and they forged an artificial relationship in the few months before the wedding.

They went shopping together.

And the bridesmaids were harvested from girls at Midwestern Accident and Life and the flower girl and ring bearer were somebody's niece and nephew and it was so apparent that our lives were some sort of façade, some sort of storybook romance without the romance and without the story.

We were like a book without any pages. We were like a book with a glossy cover that faded as soon as it was exposed to light.

And then there was the problem of guests. Deidre wanted 300. My parents wanted 300 except they were only going to pay for the rehearsal dinner and Deidre's mother wanted whatever Deidre wanted but she couldn't afford to pay for anything.

I wanted 300 because I figured my odds were better at getting laid if Deidre got what she wanted and I was getting laid more often when we first decided to get married. It was almost like old times again, Robert Palmer crooning in our bedroom as I thrust myself into Deidre trying to breathe and move in rhythm with "Some Like it Hot."

But we couldn't scratch up 300 people to invite to our wedding. We couldn't have paid 300 people to go to our wedding.

But that didn't stop Deidre and me. We planned a 300-person wedding. We put deposits down for the deejay, for the caterer with strict orders to have enough food and booze to feed and douse 300 people, and we told the banquet hall to make damn sure they had 300 chairs and place settings and enough staff to take care of us all.

And then of course we had to find a photographer, a limousine, a marriage license.

I had to get a loan to pay for it all. I had to get an advance on my year-end bonus.

We were projecting a record year in denied claims, so a good bonus wasn't going to be a problem.

And then it came time to make lists.

"You write down 150 and I'll write down 150," Deidre said. She cut her hair for the wedding because her veil would fit better. She cut it short, and her face had become too fat for short hair.

She looked like shit but I made my list. She looked like a pale peach with overgrown fuzz.

I wrote down my parents and brother. I wrote down aunts and uncles and cousins and a couple of friends from high school and college and a few co-workers at Midwestern.

I had 42 people.

Deidre had 36.

We were a long way from 300.

So we got creative. I wrote down my barber and the manager of the carwash where I got my Probe washed twice a week. Deidre invited her bank teller and the girls who did her nails and she even left an invitation for the mailman.

We would have invited the milkman if we had one.

But we did invite the clerks at the grocery store down the street from the townhouse. We handed them each an invitation as they scanned boxes of frozen dinners and weighed bunches of bananas.

They looked at us and held the invitations as if they were something somebody had stepped in.

That didn't quite get us to 200.

We invited everyone at Midwestern except the bosses because we were too afraid of the bosses, ass kissers such as ourselves. We didn't want to be embarrassed with a crappy wedding. We didn't want to embarrass ourselves in front of the middle-aged white men who held our fate in their hands.

And somehow we finally managed to invite 300 people.

But only 130 responded to the invitations.

And only 90 showed up for the wedding.

And there we were, saying our vows in front of a nearly empty church. And there we were, sitting at the reception, sitting at the head table with a sea of empty chairs and miserable faces in front of us, the misery made worse by my brother's forgettable toast, the misery made worse by the deejay playing bad dance music and his jokes in between songs that made no one laugh except my uncles and cousins who got themselves very drunk and that's what I remember the most, the really horrible part about our wedding. It was the dance floor.

No one danced.

Let me sift through the years. Let me find this one, what is it now, 2009? Things are still the same. The planet is that much hotter than it was the year before and you know this because the tulips poke through the ground in what used to be the heart of winter and you have to cut your grass earlier and earlier each year and it doesn't matter where you live. Alaska. Siberia. Greenland. You can feel the heat. You can feel the sun beat down on the back of your neck just that much more.

You can feel the burn and you know it's just a matter of years before everything goes up in smoke.

But most importantly, the enemy is still winning. The enemy is still kicking the shit out of me and I'm kicking back even though my kicks have cost me my face and the tips of my fingers.

Let's move to about a week ago. My latest hit and I think the police are zeroing in on me even though I am moving further and further out, to the other side of this state or just across the state line to cities and towns with streets I don't know.

But last week's hit was too close, *waaay* too close to home.

I have been taking it easy. There was the hit last week and a huge one last month and I am getting tired of the war but the enemy doesn't tire.

But about last month.

I found this couple at a support group meeting in the basement of a Lutheran church in Muskegon. I poured myself a Styrofoam cup of coffee and sat in a folding chair at the back of the room and the place was packed.

And these meetings are more and more packed all the time. Like I said, the enemy is striking hard, kicking the shit out me.

And they're kicking the shit out of you, even if you don't know it.

I've been to enough of these meetings to know the drill and though the people and cities are different their stories are always the same.

The people are broke and their overhead is crashing down on them.

Not everyone, of course. There are those who join support groups because they have nothing better to do. Ask anyone who's gone to AA—there's always some freak who goes because they didn't like the way they felt after a glass of wine or a beer back at a party in 1977 and they've been going to meetings *just in case...*

And that's how it is at Debtors Anonymous meetings, though usually someone who attends is up shit creek and they usually start coming to these meetings when it's too late. Any emotional support won't help them change their situation because things have spun out of control and that's how it was on this hit. There was a couple there, probably my age or a little younger. They stood in front of the room and sometimes couples are holding hands, but not this couple. They had already surrendered so they just stood there shame-faced and weary and the lady started spinning their tale. Their house was going into foreclosure and they didn't have a place to move to or anyone to move in with because all of their family was either dead or out-of-state and they had two kids, one in grade school and one in junior high, and they didn't know what to do and could anyone help them? There were some hands raised, suggestions of shelters and churches, but no one stepped up to take them in. And I know that's why they came to the meeting. They hoped people who knew their misery would sympathize and help them out but that's not DA. DA is full of people who can't take care of themselves and they aren't going to be too quick to lend a hand as their own hands are mangled and bloody and stepped on.

So I followed them home. I had to follow them closely because I was in a city that I didn't really know and I was a little nervous because the church was obviously in a rough part of town and I followed that couple in their minivan as it sped out into the suburbs and just by crossing a certain boundary road you know lives and circumstances change.

Blink and you cross a road and you pay less for auto insurance.

Blink and your kids go to better schools.

Blink and the police come when you call.

And this couple lived in a newer subdivision, not unlike all the other subdivisions you can think of, two-story houses with attached garages and lawns that are so many rolls of sod.

I watched them walk into their house.

I sat and waited and thought about burning.

We got past the wedding and got on with our lives and the marriage didn't really change us. We went on a honeymoon to the Caribbean. A cruise. Deidre had packed a bikini but wore a one-piece swimsuit instead. I wore a t-shirt with my swimsuit, even in the pool. We talked more than we fucked and we didn't talk much.

We came home, started this downward journey a little bit in love. I guess. We went on to live our life one sad and typical cliché at a time. Married, we decided to buy a house and we got a mortgage easily enough. In fact, the realtor had people lining up to give us mortgages even though our paychecks were spent before they were cashed.

And that's the first tactic of the enemy. They are more than willing to lend you money even though you know and *they* know you won't be able to pay them back, at least not in full, and definitely without spending years and years paying nothing but interest.

Interest. Lots and lots of interest. Eighteen percent here, twenty percent there and in your wallet there might be a credit card with up to twenty-nine percent interest. Usury, the bible called it.

Usury is a sin.

Punishable by fire and brimstone.

Punishable by burning.

So we bought a house in the same suburb I grew up in and I scoped it all out from work, you know, towns with the best insurance rates, the best schools, the best shopping, the best public services because you know that is all factored in on how much you have to pay in auto and home insurance. You aren't what you eat as much as you are where you live.

We bought a little brick ranch, something like 900 square feet, probably smaller than our townhouse but we were domestic. We *had* to have grass to cut, patio furniture, reasons to go to the hardware store. The mortgage wound up costing us just a little bit more than the townhouse, so that was no major stretch.

But we couldn't keep the same furniture from the townhouse. Of course not. The townhouse had more contemporary furniture, you know, a house, a home, had to be more traditional.

A plaid couch with a matching loveseat.

A wooden kitchen table with matching chairs.

A mahogany dining room table with leaves that we didn't have any room for, therefore, it was in a corner of the living room and we were constantly walking around it as we made our way to the kitchen with a matching dishwasher, stove, and refrigerator— all from Sears.

And most of our furniture came from Sears, from Sears in the mall near the office. I used a Sears credit card to pay for it all.

The Sears card got paid off last year, finally, after it all happened.

1992. Maybe 1993. I got a few more raises. I was raking in something like 40 g's a year and Deidre, down there in the phone bank, she was at 22,000.

Oh yeah, we were rich.

One problem though, we had more in expenses than we did in income. There was the wedding loan we were paying off, not to mention the Sears card, payments on my Probe and on her Grand Am, and then there were other credit cards, Deidre's, the one we both shared, the two I had on my own.

And don't forget the Amoco card for gas that I could also use at the car wash to get the Probe washed twice a week and waxed once a week along with the undercarriage rust inhibitor and the New Car air freshener.

And rust was forming along the bottom of the Probe even though I went to such lengths to prevent it.

It would be time to trade it in soon, and I went bigger the next time.

I got a Jeep. I probably went bigger because I was starting to feel smaller.

And there was a lot I didn't consider when I bought the Jeep. I didn't consider that the payments would be more than they were for the Probe. I didn't consider that it would burn more gas than the Probe and the Jeep had a bigger engine, therefore it cost more to insure.

I didn't care; I was one of the first to drive an SUV through the suburban landscape.

But still, I wasn't happy. Deidre wasn't happy, even though we got along okay. We had holes that needed filling. We had holes that we tried to fill with shopping and eating out and occasional sex and a lot of rented movies.

We were so many clichés.

And after about a year of marriage, after a year of making only minimum payments on our credit card bills and being occasionally late on other bills, Deidre said that her clock was ticking.

"I'm past thirty," she said. "On my way to forty."

And we had talked about kids. Of course we had. All couples in lust and love always talk about kids.

But we didn't want kids. At least I thought we didn't. I had ladders at Midwestern Accident and Life to climb first. We had bills to pay, stuff to buy, places to see and we often talked about travel, but we wouldn't be able to go anywhere for a long, long time because our marriage and honeymoon and new furniture and appliances put us in such a hole. A growing hole. A hole that was starting to seem bottomless.

And kids would only add to that hole. Kids would keep us tied down and I still longed for those days of doing it to music and rented pornos even though I wasn't able to keep up with the new music anymore.

I could tell the Nineties music wouldn't measure up to the Eighties at all. Grunge? Ugh.

So we didn't want kids, not for a while anyway, and Deidre had agreed.

Until she started feeling empty. Unsatisfied.

"My clock is ticking," and she listed off a number of women at Midwestern Life who had babies, stayed at home, and packed their husbands' lunches.

"I think I should stop taking the pill," she said.

"Don't do that," I said with no small amount of alarm rising in my voice. "I mean, after all, we can't afford kids, not yet, but Armstrong on the sixth floor is supposed to retire and I know I'm in the mix to replace him and that would be 45K a year and maybe then we could have kids but we'd have to get a bigger house, of course, and a station wagon or one of those minivan things and I just bought the Jeep and we owe too much on your Grand Am and don't you want to go back to the Caribbean this winter? Maybe Aruba or Grand Cayman? There are always great deals for Jamaica if you wait until March..."

Deidre held up her hand and I saw resolve in her empty blue eyes.

"I already stopped taking the pill two weeks ago," she said.

My eyes looked up in my brain and I held my breath as I searched my memory for recent sex. I realized there hadn't been any recent sex and I exhaled and even my remaining hair held in place with mousse flapped in that exhaled breeze.

"Well, you'll have to start taking them again. I know you have them..."

"I flushed them down the toilet."

And I said nothing. We had both just gotten home from work and it was a Friday night and I was loosening my tie. We hadn't had consistent sex since we got married and the sex we had was routine, straight missionary with no lights on, and Deidre only wanted to be held and kissed and I was full of so much dark wisdom from our porno days, I wanted to do it while listening to music while three women and a guy went at it on the TV screen in our bedroom and I always liked it best if one of those women wore leather or latex and carried a whip that she would only use gently.

Marriage makes women change, and it was a cliché I was living.

I shrugged my shoulders.

"It's not like we really do it anymore anyway."

And Deidre was still in her bland work clothes that she started to favor after gaining weight. She was wearing a long plaid skirt, flat shoes, a white blouse and matching plaid jacket, and her shoulder-length blonde hair was pinned up.

She nodded and let down her hair and disappeared into the bedroom.

I loosened my tie some more and went into the kitchen and grabbed a bottle of imported beer. Maybe a Heineken.

Probably an Amstel Light.

I went back into the living room and plopped my flabby ass down on the plaid couch and picked up the remote control and turned on our oversized television.

But I got nothing. We were late on the cable bill and it was shut off.

I started to get pissed but my anger subsided because Deidre strolled back into the living room wearing a lace bra and a matching garter belt and stockings that were too small. Her stomach was pinched and it hung over her garter belt and her stockings caused her thighs to swell a little but there was something so real and so sensual with the way she looked.

I thought porn star at the tail end of her career.

I felt myself get hot.

She put in a CD, a CD out of a black and dusty case.

AC/DC.

She started to dance and she shook me but not all night long.

I lasted three minutes. Maybe.

She got me hot, burning hot, and then the fire died and I was nothing but smoke and dust.

But she got me. She got me good.

Tactics.

I have to think about a change in tactics. The newspapers are full of stories every day about banks collapsing and homes going into foreclosure. Both are at an all-time high.

So what does the enemy do?

They go and lobby Congress and the president to change the bankruptcy laws. They ask for federal aid.

They make it hard for someone to go bankrupt. They just want to make you pay and pay.

And along with that they let banks double the minimum payments on credit cards, which means they're going after the weakest, those who can *only* make the minimum payment. That's how it is with any bully.

And the enemy is a bully. The enemy is the kid who pulled the wings off of butterflies. The enemy is the kid who stuck a cat in the microwave or the kid who put Bengay in someone's jock strap.

Those who are stuck making minimum payments on their credit cards can't afford to defend themselves. I couldn't defend myself until I figured out a way to strike back and that's the only way an underdog can overcome his or her suppressors. You can't fight the enemy with its own weapons.

Nor can you shoot the enemy with a gun.

Try it. See what happens. Walk up to the corporate office for Bank of America or Chase. Start firing. See what happens.

Walk up to the White House, the Capitol, some city hall. Fire bullets into the brick.

The brick will win.

You have to get creative. You have to find a new way to win the war, to play the game.

Think Boston Tea Party.

Think Hiroshima.

Think 9/11.

Tactics.

For too long I've taken care of those who were too far gone. I was taking care of the ones the enemy already bled dry. I have to get fresh blood. I have to let the enemy drink that fresh and flowing blood and then I have to shut that faucet off and let the enemy know what it feels like to be thirsty.

I am sitting in my office at the top of the Midwestern Accident and Life pyramid. I can look out my window and see miles and miles of asphalt veins cutting through a flat landscape covered with the haze of exhaust. It is morning. The sun is burning holes through the ozone and through the haze. The sunlight shines back as it reflects off of the surface of my world, reflecting off of each moving car stuck in traffic, off of each mirrored window in the office towers that surround me, reflecting off of so much glass and steel and chrome. The phone rings. The company needs me to do something, to tell an entire company that their supplemental unemployment insurance doesn't cover fire, that it doesn't help them if their place of business burns to the ground.

I do my job. I am someone's enemy. I call the head of some company or maybe their human resources manager. I don't know and it doesn't matter.

"You had flood coverage," I tell them.

"You had earthquake coverage and that was stupid of you. There aren't too many earthquakes in Michigan.

"You even had hurricane coverage. You were covered if your building was rendered useless by a swarm of locusts.

"But fire? No. Sorry.

"You had no protection from burning."

I had about three months of Deidre trying to get pregnant. Three months of doing it to music or pornos every day. Three months of pulling tricks out of my knowledge of dark wisdom and Deidre letting me do those tricks.

I could do her with her wrists tied and her mouth gagged.

I could drip hot wax on her.

She could drip hot wax on me.

I even thought about taking it a step further, you know, finding another girl to bring into our bedroom. I always wanted to see Deidre with another woman.

But I didn't have the courage to mention that.

When you come right down to it, I really am a coward.

And you would have to be a coward to let your face look like this.

But Deidre had to give in to me. She wanted to get pregnant.

So she didn't complain when I asked her to wear a platinum blonde wig and platform shoes. She didn't complain when I made her dress like a dominatrix even though we really couldn't afford the spiked boots I wanted her to get.

I have to tell you, it costs a lot of money to feed a fetish.

She wanted to get pregnant. Bad. She wanted to get pregnant and her mother was complaining because we hadn't done anything with our lives yet, let alone our marriage.

But like I said, ours was a plotless life.

She wanted to get pregnant and join that club of women who drove their kids to school and who didn't have to shower until late in the morning if at all and she wanted to be the kind of woman who didn't have to have a closet full of shoes and skirts and shirts just to make it through the week.

Her clock was ticking and mine wasn't even wound up yet.

And that three months flew. It came and went and it didn't sate me at all. It made me want more. It made me want to do more, but I didn't have a chance.

Deidre got pregnant.

She was buying one of those home testing things once a week and it was a Sunday afternoon and we had never even left the house. We stayed inside most weekends having multiple sessions of two-minute sex.

You know, sex for two minutes. Two hours to recover and then sex again.

She came out of the bathroom crying and she was wearing a pink and silk kimono and it was open and I could see her breasts sticking out suggestively and the recovery time was just about over and I was ready to go again.

But there would be none of that.

She was crying and she showed me the little stick.

"We did it," she said.

I cried too, but my tears were different.

I wasn't sure how I was supposed to react. Deidre got what she wanted and I was in love or lust with Deidre but the idea of children frightened me. I knew deep down (but not deep enough to be subconscious) that I wasn't equipped to take care of children. I could barely look after myself, let alone anyone else.

But I was happy that Deidre was happy.

But my happiness was brief. She quickly lost the silk kimono and put on sweatpants and a t-shirt and on top of that she put on a long terrycloth bathrobe and wrapped it and tied it shut.

My weekend of sex was over and things would never be the same after Deidre realized she was pregnant.

And that's not to say my life fell apart after that. I mean, I'm not entirely shallow, although I am mostly shallow.

What I mean to say is that I allowed myself some happiness after Deidre became pregnant. I wasn't planning on rejecting the child or anything like that. I was going to be responsible.

As responsible as an irresponsible person can be.

But things changed. And it's true—women change after they get married, and they change again after motherhood sets in.

And Deidre changed at the mere smell of motherhood. She didn't even wait for the baby to come.

Deidre put on that bathrobe and turned her back to me after I failed to hug her right away or show any signs of joy.

I just stood there red-faced, my cheeks burning. And I thought about fire at that point, for some reason. Flames danced in my mind only to go away.

Deidre picked up the phone to call her mother.

"She might like you now," she said as she turned the stereo off. I can't remember what was playing, maybe Duran Duran or maybe ZZ Top. I can't remember. Probably ZZ Top because of the short kimono, you know. Deidre was showing me her legs even though there was cellulite on the back of her thighs that I never acknowledged.

But the music stopped and it never really played again.

I could tell you a lot of things about what happened after Deidre got pregnant.

I could tell you that we did the responsible thing and fought the urge to sell our house right away and to buy something bigger. We kept the house because we wanted to build up some equity and we figured that a baby wouldn't take much room.

But our good moves ended there.

We spent something like, I don't know, a few thousand on baby furniture and decorating the room that was my den. The room where I kept my second stereo and stored my CDs and videotapes. And I of course wasn't one for painting or wallpaper so we hired a professional. A professional who hand-painted storks and stars and moon slices on the wall.

A professional nursery designer.

I could tell you that we did all this before Deidre even started to show, although she was already starting to gain weight. More weight.

I have to eat for two now, she said.

Another living cliché—pregnant women like to eat.

So I ate alongside her. I gained weight because she was craving pizza or pancakes every night so it was either delivery or Denny's, where you could get breakfast anytime.

Even at ten o'clock at night. This I know first-hand.

I could tell you that Deidre had to buy new clothes even before she needed maternity dresses. I could tell you that I had to buy new suits because my jackets seemed to shrink.

I could tell you I moved up a floor and was making fifty grand a year and that made a difference. Our bills didn't seem to be so insurmountable but I knew or thought that would change as soon as the baby arrived.

I could tell you that Deidre had our forthcoming child's education all planned before her first trimester was up.

"Catholic school or public school?" she asked.

I shrugged my shoulders.

"I dunno. Public school was good enough for me," I said.

"Yeah, but have you seen the test scores for our district? I mean, really, they didn't score much higher than the Detroit public schools."

And so it went. I could tell you all of that but it doesn't really shape this story. It doesn't really shape my face.

And all of the porno videotapes I bought or copied. I knew they would be of no more use to me and I wanted to change as Deidre was changing. I thought I would be happier if I changed, if I lost all of that dark wisdom. I put all of those tapes in a trash can in the back yard and burned them. The black and putrid smoke stinging my eyes and tickling my nose and I kept on hoping for flames but the flames didn't come until later and then it was a different kind of fire.

1993. Late. The house was rearranged and the baby came and Deidre's mother didn't like me any more and she may have even liked me less.

Another cliché—mothers know best.

My family was excited and my mother bought a lot of crap, you know, crap we needed, but none of that crap made me happy. Crap like diapers and baby clothes and none of it was any good to me. I couldn't eat it or drink it or wear it or listen to it and I knew I should be grateful and concerned about the welfare of my new child.

A boy, by the way. Darin.

Darin Dash.

And I was in the room when Darin was born and I was awed by the miracle of life. I was awed by the umbilical cord and the doctor gave me the scissors to cut it and I cut it with a shaking hand even though I resented what that symbolism meant.

It meant I would have to share Deidre. It meant I would have to share my life. It meant my youth was gone. Officially gone. It meant I was domesticated and kept and it meant I would have to be like my father.

Or not like my father.

And let me talk about my father, here, for a minute and only because he may explain my face, at least a little.

My father was a man of numbers. He was always talking about how much he made and he actually sold insurance, had his own agency. That's kind of how I got in with Midwestern. A phone call may or may not have been made on my behalf because my dad had been a broker for Midwestern for a shitload of years.

My dad worked a million hours a week and he was never home and when he was home he would talk to my mother at the kitchen table with a mixed drink full of ice in his hand and he would loosen his tie and tell her about all the policies he sold and how much his commission would be and how much so and so down the street made in a year and what his car was worth. His conversations were always one-sided and always about the same things; only the people and possessions changed. He talked about his brothers and sisters and cousins and how they were all scraping by and he was king of the world because his house was paid for and there was money for me and my brother to go to college.

And true enough, he paid for part of my college and that was the only way I was ever going to go. A C-minus average in high school saw to that.

But money, money was important to him. He talked about money more than he ever listened to anyone in the family. Money was an obsession for him, as were the things money could buy. New Lincoln Town Cars every couple of years. An in-ground pool in the back yard that he never seemed to have time to swim in. Jewelry for my mother that he would show off to someone whenever they had company. He would wave my mother's wrist or hand in the air and say, "This, this is the second-best cut of diamond in the world. I ordered it direct from a broker in Tel Aviv. You like it? I could get you in touch with him. He's pricey, though…"

And so it went. I learned the value of a dollar. I learned the value of hard work. It took hard work to make a dollar, and nothing was more important than a dollar. Not even family.

And I know I sound heavy handed and sentimental here, but that is how I remember my father. I remember him for his new cars and slicked back hair and cufflinks. I remember his perpetual absence and I remember the last time I saw him, slumped in his chair in his office. Business was bad by then; all of his old customers had died and there weren't enough new ones to take their place. I remember his face, they way it shined just before it disappeared in flames and turned to ash.

If you have kids or had kids then you know what I went through with Darin and Deidre. I won't bore you with the nocturnal feedings and the crying and teething and the streams of soiled diapers.

Now, someone like me, full of desire that didn't go away in smoke and a love of music, would have been miserable stuck in a house with a disinterested and exhausted stay-at-home wife and a baby that still had no personality and cried and shit and pissed all of the time.

I should have been miserable. I expected to be miserable.

But I wasn't.

I thought things would get tougher, financially, with Deidre not working even though she did have maternity benefits from Midwestern but they ran out after Darin was a month old and Deidre had no plans to go back to work.

She was what she always wanted to be: a mother. A thirty-one-year-old mother with an executive husband and a house of her own.

She baked cookies, even though there was no one around to eat them, really.

"Darin will appreciate this someday," she said, of her young son, our young son, who was still a long way from teeth and solid food.

But things actually got easier, financially. Deidre not working actually cost less than her working because she didn't need to get a new pair of shoes every other week to match the skirt or purse she got the week before and there was no more going out to eat six or seven times a week because it was too much of a hassle taking the baby out so we were stuck buying groceries like average people and we ate at the kitchen table or in front of the TV like average people and I was actually starting to make headway on our bills. I was starting to get caught up on our credit cards and the car payments weren't breaking our backs anymore because we sold her Grand Am. She didn't need it anymore. She didn't go anywhere, and if she had to go to the doctor or somewhere during the day she would just drive me to work in the Jeep.

And you're probably wondering how I kept all that dark wisdom at bay. You're probably wondering how I kept all those fetishes in check since my desires could no longer be satisfied.

Well, it was easy.

I was too tired. Deidre was too tired. Darin, like every other baby, I'm sure, never slept through the night. Deidre was the one who got up with him but I of course woke up too, even if only for a moment. I never got a good or full night's sleep and it's amazing how little you care about certain things when you're sleep deprived. My sleep deprived cock barely ever rose and I usually wanted to eat all the time while I was at work, you know, sugar to stay awake. Colas full of caffeine, fast-food burgers full of fat and sodium.

I gained weight. I gained more weight and I figured I could eat and drink all I wanted because I had that lifetime membership at the gym but I was always too tired to go to the gym and if I wasn't too tired then Deidre wanted me home to help with Darin so that's how my life went and it wasn't horrible. It's amazing how much money you save when you do nothing and I was content with that. A certain restlessness was taken out of me and I tried to be a good and nurturing father. I read to Darin because that's what all the parenting magazines said to do even if he was too young to understand. So we stocked his bookshelves with all the cliché children's books. Cat in the Hat. Green Eggs and Ham. Goodnight Moon. Where the Wild Things Are. The Owl and the Pussycat.

And my favorite, My World, especially some of the opening lines.

The fire burns. The pages turn.

I thought of those lines later. I wasn't drawn to them in those early days; they were just words, all part of the babble that came out of my mouth as I read to my son.

I tried. I was fat and tired and I tried.

But I couldn't stay decent for long. Darin soon turned two and the sleep became more regular and I wasn't so exhausted anymore. I started walking on my lunch breaks and I probably cut a ridiculous figure.

Picture a pear-shaped man walking along a sidewalk in between office buildings and a shopping mall. Picture a sidewalk that no one ever actually walks on and picture that sidewalk along six lanes of traffic.

I wasn't embarrassed. I was struggling too much to be embarrassed. The finances were pretty much in order but my body was wrecked and I was still vain and my reflection and cast shadow bothered me more than my fiscal life.

Now, I don't want you to think I was rolling in it, but I was able to pay all my bills including the mortgage and car payment and I still had money left over at the end of the month and that hadn't happened in a long time.

But there were still bills. A lot of bills. If I lost my job or even a week's salary, I would be screwed. I would be drowning in a sea of debt. A sea with no bottom.

But I was managing and feeling pretty good about my future. I even started a little retirement fund through Midwestern, I got my first life insurance policy, and I thought about a college fund for Darin.

But I didn't think about it for very long. I figured I'd better make sure my future was secure before I started worrying about somebody else.

Even if that somebody else was my son. My own flesh and blood.

The fire in my eyes.

Yeah, I know what you're thinking. I'm a selfish bastard. But I also figured my father would take care of his grandchild even though he didn't show much of an interest in Darin. My father lived about ten minutes away and we maybe saw him once every two months in the first two years of Darin's life.

It's just how it is.

It's just how it was.

But then Darin got a little older and a little less needy and I started sleeping better and a rested body bears a restless mind and urges started coming on. I wanted to start having sex again but Deidre wasn't ready for sex and wasn't willing for sex and when she finally did give in the sex was far from torrid and satisfying. I was so hell bent on having good sex that I would last about a minute and a half and that was it. And the sex was always in the dark with no music and nothing on the TV and I regretted burning all those porno tapes.

So I had to find an outlet.

Now mind you, this was before the internet explosion, before so much sex exploded across computer screens. Let's face it, you can satisfy any urge you might have just by typing in the Google search bar.

Try typing *fat naked pissing and farting girls*.

Try typing *wheelchair orgasm*.

Go ahead.

I didn't have that luxury. I didn't have so much available so easily.

I had to work for it.

I had to find it.

And meanwhile, while those urges were growing and burning in my soul, Deidre gave me some news.

She was pregnant again.

It's 2009 again, maybe still.

I had to fire somebody, someone in my staff, a nice young boy out of college who just bought his first car and who just made a deposit on his first apartment and I have to tell you, even though he started at a salary forty percent higher than my starting salary, an apartment costs twice as much now as it did back then, even though the area around the office and the shopping mall is starting to crumble. The shiny office towers just aren't so shiny anymore and the urban sprawl is spreading like a fungus across this corner of the state.

And the fungus leaves a residue of slime in its wake.

Take a look at our city or any major city. The downtown is probably fixed up and hip enough for Starbucks and nightclubs, but I guarantee you the neighborhoods are in shambles.

It started with expressways and then it started with sprawl. Webs of traffic and cars and SUVs and unleaded gasoline.

And the sprawl covered my suburb, my subdivision, and now it looks slimed over. The streets are crumbling in some places with cracks and potholes. The sidewalk in front of my house is starting to buckle because the trees along my street that used to be mere splinters when I first moved in are starting to uproot it.

So I could have felt bad for this young boy who put gel in his hair and worked all the hours his salary required and then some.

But I don't feel bad for anyone.

I had to fire him because he wasn't firm enough with clients. He was too lenient in his claims.

At Midwestern, no means no.

At Midwestern, the customer is never right.

He was approving too many claims and eating into our profits.

And my monthly bonus is based on profit.

The more the company keeps, the more I make.

Capitalism. Greed. It's what makes it all go.

It's what made my family go.

I tried to salvage him. I tried to toughen him up, but he didn't have it in him. Some crying old lady would get him on the phone and her tears would ruin him. He felt sorry for people. He had compassion and all of that bullshit that gets you nowhere in this world.

Nowhere except out of a real job with a real company to passing out coffee in a shopping mall to teenagers and housewives.

I fired him.

And I wasn't sorry to see him go.

Deidre got pregnant again and I recall the night it happened so perfectly because it was so awful. The bedroom was dark and I climbed on top of her and pulled up her ankle length nightgown and she said no but I didn't listen and I forced myself inside her and my mind was full of so many images, old porn movies and a new girl on the second floor of Midwestern who had a big ass and liked to wear tight skirts. I started thrusting and I heard Deidre moan just a little and I came and that was it.

She got pregnant.

And she glowed in motherhood and expectant motherhood and I knew her body of just a few years prior was gone to never be seen again and I had already stopped loving Deidre by this point. The lust was gone and I was burning with lust and I had to find a place to burn it.

I couldn't burn it with Deidre, and Darin and the coming baby were just in my way, even though I probably loved Darin at that point. Maybe.

I was never going to become Parent of the Year.

So I had to find an outlet. I'd never been a ladies' man despite my penchant for sex and pornography.

Or probably because of it.

I really had no idea how to pick up women. Deidre and I just sort of collapsed into each other. We got stuck together and we felt comfortable in our self-inflicted misery and desire.

We were pretty much made for each other, like the clichés go.

But parenthood didn't change me the way it changed Deidre. Not in the long run.

So I had to find an outlet.

I wanted to get laid.

Now, I'm sure you're thinking why not jerk off, because, let's face it, everybody jerks off.

I was doing that anyway, but jerking off is like chewing gum still in the wrapper. You get to chew something, but it's not the same.

Or it's like light beer or skim milk or buying a brand new *used* car. I could come up with a hundred analogies.

You get my point. Maybe you've felt my point.

But what did you do about it?

If you're smart, you did nothing.

Darin was three, almost four, so this had to be late 1996 or early '97. Deidre was expecting and I was a star at Midwestern.

Deidre wanted to buy a bigger house.

I wanted to get laid.

Deidre was wondering what school district we should move into.

I was wondering if I'd ever see Deidre in a garter belt again and if not Deidre, then who?

Well, a pregnant Deidre wasn't about to wear a garter belt. A pregnant and maternal Deidre had zippo interest in sex and sex was all I thought about even at work and I became a real prick at work and I even asked one of the new phone bank girls if she wanted to go to lunch because I heard she had slept with some of the younger guys in the lower floors.

She looked at my hair and laughed.

I knew I couldn't pick up women with my charm or looks or animal magnetism. I had and have the charisma of a fish. A dead and decaying fish. So I knew I had to use the only thing that ever worked for me.

Money.

I figured I'd go find a hooker.

I thought it would be easy enough.

I thought I'd leave the suburbs and drive into the city and there the hookers would be just waiting for business. I had it all worked out. I would find one that looked not too worn out but one that looked a little bit desperate, desperate enough to do whatever I wanted and my mind was full of so many things, mostly of an S&M bent, with me falling beneath each one of those letters at some point.

I don't want to bore you with my fantasies or my perversions.

But it's not like hookers carry neon signs. It's not like hookers work in storefronts.

I drove around.

I drove around some of the crappiest parts of Detroit, parts of the city I didn't even know existed. It's amazing—I've lived less than half an hour away from the city for most of my life and I don't know it all. I felt like I was a world away from the Michigan I know. I drove through parts of the city full of abandoned houses and factories and boarded up storefronts. I drove through parts of the city where people just stood on the sidewalk doing nothing except breathing and staring at a pudgy white dude driving a Jeep.

So I didn't find any hookers that way.

I found them much easier than that.

You can find them too, if you try. Just check the classified section of your local paper, that is, if you live in a big city. There's always a section for dating services.

There you go.

That's where the hookers are and I'm sure the cops know it and I'm not here to debate the will of law enforcement.

I don't give a fuck about law enforcement and they didn't give a fuck about me for the longest time.

They could have stopped me a long time ago if they had really wanted to.

They could have stopped me if they had really tried. They could have stopped me if they had opened their eyes. After all, I only left about a million clues.

I'm leaving clues still.

Anyway, you're probably wondering what the point to all this is. Why am I telling you about hookers and cops and clues?

The point is there is no point.

All of this is pointless. My whole life has been pointless. Meaningless.

And you're probably wondering how someone with children could think his life is meaningless.

It just is. Children happen. They don't change a man, especially when he doesn't want to be changed.

So I spent a lot of nights meeting massage and escort girls in hotel rooms near the office. I paid for the massages with a credit card and the extras I paid with cash.

I got the cash from advances on my credit card. You gotta love the ATM.

Darin was starting pre-school and changing every day and Deidre's stomach was starting to swell with our forthcoming child and I was getting handcuffed and beaten in some hotel room or in some nondescript and sterile apartment. I was wearing a leather mask or I was making it with two girls at the same time and I started getting girls at least once a week and after about three months it was a twice a week and I started running into the same girls again.

After all, there isn't an infinite supply of pretty young girls willing to let fat balding thirty-somethings drool saliva and sperm all over them.

It wasn't enough. The sex wasn't enough. The girls weren't enough and my money wasn't going far enough.

I didn't pay the mortgage during Deidre's ninth month of pregnancy and the bank called her at the house looking for money, telling her our house could be taken away.

She cried and went into labor and our daughter Sarah was born.

I fucked strange girls on Tuesday and Thursday nights and I gave Deidre a lot of excuses and she bought all of them.

I told her I was working late. I told her I joined a bowling league. I told her I joined a golfing league.

I told her we had to cut back on groceries for a while. I told her that I wasn't getting bonuses because there had been too many claims lately and that's why money was tight but that wasn't true.

I was doing great at work, denying claims and having a grand old time.

But I was broke. Broke and miserable and it took me a while to figure out why I was miserable. I thought it could have been because I was starting to get tied down to family life even though a guy who picks up hookers twice a week with his very pregnant wife and toddler son still at home isn't exactly tied down.

I should have been happy, having sex any way I wanted.

Or any way I could afford.

And that's what made me miserable. I could tell none of these girls liked me. I was nothing more than their job, a couple of bucks. I was probably repulsive to them and I could see it in their eyes when they thought I wasn't looking and even when I was looking. There's really nothing more shameful than having someone stare at you with disgust after you pull your condom wrapped dick out of them.

So, after a while, I wasn't happy.

I wasn't happy and Sarah's first year was a blur. I remember one Saturday night with an escort girl in a hotel near the airport and then Sunday morning at church singing hymns and getting Sarah baptized.

And then Monday came and it was time to deny claims and make money.

Let's move through years. I can do that because so many years were meaningless. Let's move up three years or so, the late Nineties. Things were great at Midwestern as people were making more money than they deserved and policies were being sold at a rapid clip and bonuses were passed out monthly and I moved up a couple of floors and we entered the first part of the century. Let's take a look at my family.

Darin and Sarah are growing and they're doing well enough and they seem so very average. Average intelligence and average looks and they lead average suburban lives. They eat cereal for breakfast every morning in front of the TV and then Deidre takes them to school in a leased minivan and that's how we started to do it.

We leased vehicles instead of bought them because the monthly payments were lower and we could get something new every couple of years and the vehicles I drove always matched my status at Midwestern. First there was a Taurus, then a Lincoln and then a couple of Cadillacs and then another Mustang when I became obsessed with youth again.

I can tell you this—a car might make a man, but it doesn't change a man.

So we leased vehicles and Deidre went through minivans and I went through sedans and I gave up on the escort girls. I loved the sex but I hated the loathing and there were two kids at home and Deidre was getting wise to the bowling league excuse.

"How come you don't own your own ball yet?"

I shrugged my shoulders and gave up on the escort girls and turned my attention to Deidre and girls at Midwestern. I started to hit on the new hires but not the real pretty ones. I had to stay within my means and it took a while to learn how to talk to them but I figured it out and I was also able to do this, not because I was still old and fat and bald but because I'd moved up high enough in the company and I had two things going for me when I hit on these girls—I had status and fear. I would let them sink into the leather of my Cadillac and then I'd put the moves on them, tell them I could help their careers.

Sometimes I got slapped and sometimes I scored and sometimes I got reprimanded by one of the big bosses who would kind of wink at me because he pulled the same shit himself over the years and the girls who complained were given small raises or else some bullshit excuse was found to fire them. And even if they found a lawyer, so what? Any lawyer they could hire couldn't match the firepower of a Midwestern lawyer on retainer.

Midwestern loved me. Loves me still.

And Deidre, I'd buy her flowers every once in a while, and I'd tell her I have needs and we'd do it after the kids went to bed. We'd do it with all the lights off in our bedroom and it'd be quick and almost joyless and it still wasn't enough.

I craved sex all the time.

I craved sex and shopping and despite my salary increases our bills continued to mount.

Mortgage and lease payments and paying for your dry-cleaning with a credit card will do that to you, that and me signing up for every pay-per-view porn site on the internet.

We of course had to move after Sarah was born. We had to move to some far-flung suburb of new subdivisions of oversized houses and good schools. We left our neighborhood of small houses and towering trees and exchanged it for one full of towering houses and small trees. Our old neighbors were plumbers and mechanics and salesmen and our new neighbors were doctors and lawyers and salesman and guys like me, mid-level corporate executives who liked to play golf on the weekend.

Our new neighborhood was our family replicated a thousand times.

Everyone had two or three kids and the wives drove minivans and the husbands drove oversized sedans or SUVs and everyone's living room was furnished with white furniture that was never used while the "great rooms" were full of oversized couches and oversized TVs. Imagine living in a place where everyone is just like you, where every house is a mirror of your own.

It's becomes a slow hell.

A burning hell.

Competition.

I've always loved competition. I loved competing with the guys at Midwestern, especially the guys I hired in with. It didn't take me long to figure out what the company wanted—to make it above the first floor and on to the second and the third.

The fourteenth floor is where I am now, and I can't get any higher even if I become CEO or a member of the board. My salary is now six figures and six figures should go a long way after you've literally burned yourself out.

I got into running after I gave up the escort girls. But I just didn't get into running, I jumped into it. I ran at least five miles a day and entered marathons and 10Ks.

I went from one addiction to another and the running gave me reasons to shop.

I had to buy certain running shoes, certain running shorts, socks, watches, heart rate monitors, magazines, and food.

I got thin and athletic and then the Mustang came back as did some of the girls in the lower floors and they started to come a hell of a lot easier. I had status and fear and no gut.

I even started going back to the gym.

And my sudden athleticism made Deidre feel awkward. She was afraid I was exercising just to make myself attractive to other women.

And that was true. I never wore my wedding ring away from home or Deidre's eyes, but I had no plans to leave her, not in those days. Those ideas didn't come to me till later, near the end, when things got out of control.

So that was my life for a number of years. Running, competing against myself and my miles per minute, going from twelve minutes a mile to seven and a half at my peak.

And there was shopping, wooing girls on the first floor of Midwestern and being known around the office as a pig or a lucky son of a bitch.

It all depended on who you asked.

But I had to keep Deidre happy at home too. Divorce rarely crossed my mind and when it did I knew it wouldn't fit in with my lifestyle. I would have to cut everything in half and then pay child support and alimony and that would make me live in some crummy apartment despite my then high-five-figure salary.

So no, divorce was never an option.

Deidre and I were birds of a feather, easily addicted to fads and pleasure and Deidre became addicted to her life, her stay-at-home soccer mom life, and you may think that's silly, but there's a lot of money and advertising aimed at the stay-at-home mom.

Deidre knew a lot of the people in our subdivision, as well as the other moms at school.

She was involved in the PTA and other groups that she told me about in great detail as we were lying in our darkened bedroom each night with only the glow of a muted TV to illuminate us.

She told me all about the teachers and the other parents and the clubs and the PTA committees and there were always small checks needed for this and that and I gave her the checks. I'd leave them on the kitchen counter in the morning, usually on the granite-topped mahogany island that we had installed when Sarah was two.

Competition. Our house was barely two years old and we were the first in our subdivision to have our kitchen remodeled. We called a 1-800 number from a television commercial and financed the remodeling. We got the granite-topped mahogany island and chrome appliances and Deidre ordered all new pots and pans and silverware from one of the shopping channels. The pots and pans were hung above the island and immediately began to gather dust and they are hanging there still, like effigies of remembrance and some of the chrome got singed in the fire and I could have claimed it on my insurance but I'm not really that greedy. The renovation of my house after the fire cost Midwestern enough.

Competition.

The police are driving past my house every day now and sometimes the cars are marked but usually they are unmarked and I know I have all kinds of law enforcement are looking at me, trying to figure me out.

Local, state, federal.

There is no fire now, but a fire still burns.

Competition.

First the remodeled kitchen. Then came the Florida room on the back of the house.

Another year or two passed. I can't remember the timeline exactly as my memories are blurred by monthly payments and quickies in the back of my car and hotel rooms near the mall.

But there was competition.

Inspired by Deidre and me, other neighbors had their kitchens remodeled and porches and massive decks built on to the back of their houses. And then there were those who had their yards professionally landscaped with automatic sprinklers and in-ground lights operated by timers.

We did all of that.

We did all of that and then we trumped everyone.

We got a pool. And not a flimsy above-ground pool, either. That does nothing but kill your grass.

No.

We got a kidney-shaped full-sized pool with a diving board and we had our deck extended out to the pool and around the pool we poured a patio that is still there, a mix of concrete and brick inlays shaped like stars and moons.

Oh yeah.

Deidre envisioned having lots of guests.

But that never happened.

We really couldn't afford to entertain after the pool. That and no one in the neighborhood really seemed to like us. That and I was out all the time, working late, chasing girls, and running in 10Ks and half-marathons.

And Darin and Sarah? You know, I don't even remember what they looked like back then. I remember that guilt would sometimes make me stay home until 9pm, long enough for me to tuck them into bed and kiss them goodnight. I would then go back downstairs with Deidre and I would stretch my arms and yawn and say, "I guess I'll be going now," and I would give Deidre some bullshit story about meeting a potentially new and huge client at the airport, how the bosses wanted someone from the upper floors to pick that person up, take them around town and show them a good time.

"Oh," Deidre would say and she didn't seem to care. She didn't seem to care as long as the stuff kept coming, as long as the pool got cleaned and the grass cut and the payments on her minivan kept getting made.

Competition.

We were competing already and we thought we were winning. I thought I was winning, anyway. I really don't know what Deidre thought in those days.

But really, we were already starting to lose.

There were a lot of bullshit days and if you strung them together you got a lot of crappy years. I got sick of running and started something else. I got into wine tasting.

I got into wine. I got into golf.

I got into martial arts and yoga. I got into meditation and Buddhism. You'd be shocked how many books there are about Buddhism that all say basically the same thing.

Nirvana. I was looking for nirvana and I'm looking for it still and I'm not even close to it. But now I feel all right because I'm making a difference.

I've made a difference.

I've made a sad difference and that difference is staring me back in the face as I look in the mirror to brush my teeth, teeth that look like stars in a black and ash marble sky.

Nirvana.

I bought a lot of shit, a lot of books and food and you would think something somewhat decent like an interest in Buddhism would make me a better father or parent.

But you would be wrong.

Because it wasn't really Buddhism I was interested in. True, I was searching for nirvana, happiness, fulfillment, but that had nothing to do with Buddhism.

It had to do with the stuff that went along with it.

Think about it.

Think about the next time you go shopping for something. Anything. A car, for example. You want to project an image. Let me throw clichés at you.

Clichés that you will catch.

Let's just pretend that you're a twenty-five-year-old male who lives in a rural area. Let's pretend you like to hunt and fish and you chew tobacco and you only like country music and the only things you collect are guns and girlfriends and you probably have more of the former.

Let's pretend money is no object.

You aren't going to drive a Hyundai. Or a Subaru or an Audi or a Cadillac.

You just won't.

You'll probably drive a truck of some sort. A big Chevy or Ford. Loaded. Full of leather and chrome and speakers.

You can throw any type of person at me and I can tell you what kind of car they definitely *won't* drive. You can too. Find a profession, a race, an income level, and you can match the car to the person. It's not hard. Soccer moms, busboys without green cards, carpet salesmen (a Dodge Intrepid, less than eight years old if they're lucky or good), construction workers, young doctors, old doctors.

Insurance executives without a conscience and an insatiable appetite for lust and stuff.

And so it goes. Cars, music, furniture, houses, clothes, silk sheets, lingerie, books, breakfast cereal, beer... you name it. We all buy products that project an image we want the world to see. I even learned about that in college, but I forget the class. It might have been Marketing 101.

I've learned and I've lived it and the closest thing to nirvana Deidre and I ever experienced wasn't love or sex or the birth of our children.

The birth of our children wasn't even close. The birth of our children brought on a change in our spending habits. The birth of our children was a handcuff.

We were happiest when we were shopping, buying stuff for the house and ourselves, sitting with a contractor as he designed our new kitchen and Florida room while sitting in our living room. We were happiest forking over a thousand-dollar check to the contractor as a deposit even though that left us with eleven dollars in our bank account.

We didn't care.

Credit cards would see us through.

Times change. Things change. Stuff changes.

Let's take recent history, for example. The Nineties as they progressed to this century. You probably have an internet connection and a cell phone and probably an iPod.

You have them, I have them, most Americans living above the poverty level have them.

Even people below the poverty level have these things. I've seen them. I've driven past cramped apartment buildings and trailer parks with runny nosed kids in dirty clothes playing along the side of the road with a satellite dish attached to the roof of their trailer or out some apartment window with a blanket for a curtain. And sometimes the kids are watched by some fat mother talking on her cell phone as she barely pays attention to her kid from some second- or third-story window or some half-assed porch attached to a trailer.

Trailers. I've hit a couple of trailers and it's not the fire or smoke inside a trailer that will get you.

It's the heat.

Anyway, stuff.

Stuff that wasn't available in the Nineties. I remember driving around looking for a payphone trying to call girls or work or Deidre when I was out prowling.

Well, not prowling. I couldn't really catch anything unless I paid for it somehow. Even the girls at Midwestern, I mean, they weren't with me because of my looks, they were with me because of the floor I was on. They wanted something in return, even though they would never admit it.

Stuff. I thought I was hot shit with my Mustangs and stereos and VCRs and people would laugh at me now if that's all I had.

You have to have stuff, but how much?

Well, I have to tell you, it's never enough.

There are certain things you need to live the life Deidre and I led. You need to have a certain income, something between 75 and

125 thousand a year. That should do it. That should be enough to establish and apply for and receive all the credit you could possibly need, somewhere in the hundreds of thousands of dollars.

And then you have to spend. You have to spend and pay and spend and pay. Your country needs this from you. It's more patriotic than flying an American flag from your front porch. It's what keeps the country spinning on its axis of plastic and usury.

Think about it.

Think if people stopped spending money. Think if they stopped going to the malls and grocery stores on weekends. Think if they spent their money on other things.

What other things?

Exactly.

There are no other things.

I took up cigars and scotch to go along with golf. Deidre took up scrapbooking and photography and genealogical research and spice collecting.

Surprise. We are all descended from Europeans who came to the New World to forge a better life in the miles and miles of wilderness and swamps that gave way to settlements and churches that gave way to main streets and factories and office towers that gave way to subdivisions and shopping malls and suburbs and patriotism and war and blood and oil and money coming in and a lot more going out.

Debt.

This all has to do with debt.

Let's take a look at golf.

You can drop a hundred bucks easy on a round of golf and that doesn't count the membership fees or the thousand you spent on clubs and balls and gloves and jackets and those satiny slacks that ripple in the wind and you like to think you're at Pebble Beach but really you're in suburban Detroit and no one gives a damn if you par or not except the buddy from work you're golfing with and that's only because you have money riding on each hole.

Five bucks here, twenty bucks there. Cigars in the cart, drinks in the clubhouse, and this is some form of fellowship. I remember when Deidre and I tried to go to church for a little while when Darin was first born. There was a men's club and prayer breakfasts and it was all for fellowship. Another way to make friends.

Fellowship. Friends. More competition and that's all friends really are or at least that's all they've ever been for me, at least in my adult life. Sure, when I was a kid there were friends, fellow misfits who I had sleepovers with in grade school, who I shared glimpses of porno mags with in junior high, and who I drank beer and smoked weed with in high school, and my friends and I were the kind of guys who didn't get girls. It just wasn't going to happen then or there, just as there were girls who were boyfriendless, but everybody finds somebody sooner or later.

And sometimes that somebody ruins your life.

Or you ruin their life.

Or you ruin a life together.

Or in my case, a whole lot of lives.

Friends. My misfit high school friends. There was no competition, just birds of a feather, just miserable company who talked about how great our lives would be after high school, after we got out of our miserable and dying and dirty-white-collar suburb.

We had dreams. We went to college. Girls finally did come. Money came. Possessions and stuff came.

The dreams died.

I was going to be a stockbroker. That's what I was going to be. I was going to go to Wall Street and kick ass, but Midwestern hired me out of college almost right at the job fair before I even nosed around anywhere else. Midwestern picked me out of that mediocre crowd of graduates with bachelor degrees in business.

Business with a minor in marketing. How fucking original is that?

I got original later, after so many years of denying claims, protecting the Midwestern assets because a dollar saved for the company was half a penny in my pocket, or maybe one hundredth of a penny but that doesn't matter because my pockets got stuffed with the fruits of denied claims and those fruits burned a hole through my wallet, through my pocket and they burned the rest of my life.

Golf.

I was playing shitty, hacking away, the ball going all over the place, but I wouldn't back down from the guy I was playing with. His name was Reece and he had a hot little wife that I wanted to fuck and I would stare at her and try to steer her into a corner during office Christmas parties or after work get-togethers that included the wives. Reece's wife, Tara or Tanya, always wore tight sweaters with plunging necklines and she had a rack on her and she always showed off her cleavage and there is no way in hell those tits were real because her ass and waist were so narrow and small.

And let's face it, you've never seen a woman, a real woman, less than five and a half feet tall and 120 pounds with a thin waist and no ass sport a set of C-cup tits.

It just doesn't happen.

So we were golfing, Reece and I, and there was cigar smoke and cans of beer in our golf bags and we were playing eighteen holes and I bogeyed or double bogeyed every hole and Reece shot a ten over and by the time it was done I was three hundred bucks in debt.

"Pay the man," Reece said as we loaded our clubs into the golf cart, drunkenly weaving our way back to the clubhouse.

"Sorry bud, no cash. I'll have to square with you later." I never had any cash. Why bother with cash when you're flush with plastic? Why bother with cash when you've reached a point in your life where the money comes and then it goes the minute it comes like a high tide that lasts no more than a nanosecond?

"All right, you can start with buying me my fucking dinner. I can probably eat enough steak and drink enough scotch and beer to eat up half of your tab."

I said fine. I phoned Deidre to tell her I wouldn't be home for dinner and I heard Darin and Sarah fighting in the background and I have to tell you, I never remember my house being particularly happy. No one was glad to see anyone come or go and there weren't a lot of hugs or kissing.

But I didn't notice that then. I was on fire and I was fanning the flames.

Reece and I went to a restaurant near the office because ghosts always return to their favorite haunts and nothing in the suburbs choked with people and exhaust and misery is really far away. I drove my Cadillac and Reece followed me in his Audi and I was jealous of his Audi for a moment. I felt like an old man driving that Cadillac and I thought of Reece's wife in a white fur coat sprawled naked in the passenger seat of the Audi, her legs bare and spread open against the black leather seat...

We ate at a Japanese place, a favorite lunch place for Midwestern executives on the upper floors. I ordered two plates of sushi as an appetizer and the beer and food flowed along with sake and scotch and we talked about the office and business and how shitty my golf game was that day and we laughed and had a great time and I had no clue the bottom was about to fall.

An hour came and went. We stared at all the women walking in and out of the restaurant and it didn't matter if the women were attached to husbands or boyfriends or even trailing kids behind them.

We pointed, stared, and laughed and we got a lot of glares from men and women alike.

It came time to pay and the bill was close to two hundred bucks. I pulled out my wallet and took out a credit card, a Chase

Bank Visa, one with twenty-one percent interest and my minimum monthly payment was like four hundred bucks.

You could and can buy or lease a car for four hundred bucks a month. A halfway decent car. Maybe, shit, I don't know. I don't have to worry about that stuff anymore.

I gave the waitress my credit card. I felt pretty good, my face warm and flush with booze and laughter, and without thinking I put the card inside the leather bill holder that nicer restaurants like to give you so your tab can be discreet, so you feel no shame by blowing a day's worth of wages on appetizers and booze and a meal prepared by strange hands, hands that wipe asses and other things.

The Chase card. It had a ten thousand dollar limit and I knew I was hovering close to the maximum. I figured I had like eight grand on it or so, and what's eight grand? Well, to me it was golf clubs and cigars and car washes and full tanks of only the highest octane.

There was that and coffee from the Starbucks down the street from the office and everyone from the office congregated at Starbucks in the morning, standing in line, tapping our feet, and it was the place to make sure the new pair of shoes or tie or purse or whatever got noticed, before you got to the office and found yourself drowning in keyboard strokes and fluorescent lighting and yeah, I used the credit card to pay for my coffee.

Why the hell not?

The waitress came back, a little Mexican chick I probably would have made a pass at but having my balls handed to me on a platter on the golf course kind of took the wind out of my libido and I wanted to ask her why a Mexican like her was working in a Japanese restaurant. I knew that most of the staff was Filipino, at least an attempt to hire Asians, but a Mexican...

"Sorry, sir," she said. Her name was Rosalie and it's funny how you remember vividly the pivotal moments in your life. I remember Reece grinning at me with his red and drunk face glowing underneath his Titleist ball cap.

"I'm sorry, but your card was declined," and the word declined coming from her lips really stung because of the way it sounded with her accent.

Dee-kleined.

I felt my heart stop. I felt sweat start to build on the back of my neck and I have to tell you, that's the first time I ever felt real fear or stress or discomfort in my life. Sure, I've been pissed off before. I've felt slighted because the service was bad at some restaurant or when I've been cut off in traffic or when I've found my Cadillac with a ding in the door left by some asshole who parked too close to me.

And the kids. I used to get mad at the kids all the time, especially on Sunday mornings when I wanted to sleep some hangover off. They'd play in front of a blaring TV, the sounds of their screams and laughter mixing with some cartoon music creating a cacophony of sound that would drift up the stairs and enter my pounding and nauseous head. I would storm down the stairs and turn the TV off and yell at them so loud that Sarah would start to cry and Deidre would come running from the kitchen and hug her tightly and say Daddy needs his rest, he's got a hell of a week ahead of him and I remember one morning after two hookers, my balls aching as they hung suspended in my boxer shorts as I stood like a madman in the great room, my two kids staring at me like I was a stranger, and I didn't care.

I used to get really pissed at Midwestern when someone beneath me didn't do their job right and approved one claim more than they were allowed. That's how it goes; Midwestern puts a limit on the amount of claims one can approve without approval from upper management.

I don't get pissed anymore. I just stare, and that's scary enough.

I pulled off my Nike cap and scratched my head and pretended to be aloof.

"Wow, it should work."

"You want I try again?"

"Yeah," I said, "try it again. It's probably just a glitch."

I learned later that credit card companies don't have glitches.

She tried it again.

"It still no work," she said.

At this point I was embarrassed and pissed but not afraid. I had a slew of cards in my wallet. I had two credit cards for every picture of my kids and I had four pictures of Darin and Sarah and I never looked at them, never showed them off unless someone asked.

I put the Nike hat back on and said son-of-a-bitch and Reece started to dig for his wallet and I knew that piece of shit had enough cash in his wallet to cover everything.

"Need some help?"

"Fuck no," I said and I handed the waitress my American Express card. Platinum.

I remember how fucking great I thought I was when I got that card. I thought I was somebody, an official member of the upper class.

Let's face it; the kid at the drive-thru window at McDonald's doesn't have an American Express platinum card.

I gave Reece a frustrated and pissed-off look as if to say what-the-fuck or I'm-sorry-about-that.

"Deidre must have used that card up," I said to explain everything, but I kept Deidre on a pretty short leash. She only had three credit cards and I never questioned her bills, I just paid them as they came due.

I laughed as the waitress walked away and I took a swig of my now warm Amstel Light.

But the laughter was gone. Reece just sat there staring at me drinking his probably warm Heineken.

"Sorry sir, this no work either."

This time I got angry. I called her a stupid cunt. I called her a stupid and stinking wetback slut.

"What do you mean it doesn't fucking work?" I yelled and this time the manager came over, a short and fat Filipino dude with a thin and wispy mustache with his thinning hair parted to the side. He was dressed in some sort of smock with Japanese writing on it and I was looking for a sword inside his sash.

If there was a sword I would have grabbed it and killed myself because I knew the waitress wasn't deserving of my anger. I knew that I was starting to lose my grip on the life that I knew because each month was getting tougher and tougher to keep the bills straight and the payments on time.

I knew why the American Express card wouldn't work. It was because I was late on the bill and to play ball with American Express you *have to be on time*. American Express doesn't have time for any penny ante bullshit. You either pay or you're out.

I was out and I was pissed.

I took out my wallet and threw the rest of my credit cards at the manager—find one that works or else get your fucking equipment checked.

Reece looked at me, shook his head, and drained his beer.

"I gotta go," he said. "You sure you don't need some cash?"

"No," I said. "Go home and fuck your wife for me."

He looked at me kind of funny, kind of like he wanted to kick my ass or something but then he realized I was a floor above him even though right then and there I felt like I was miles below him and every other creature walking on the face of the earth.

He said, "Yeah, sure, I'll tell her you said hi. Don't worry about the rest of the money you owe me."

And that stung and I was left there with the entire place staring at me. I felt my face burn and I thought about spontaneous combustion. I thought I could will myself to catch on fire. That would give the folks something to stare at.

It took a combination of four credit cards to pay my bill. I knew I was getting bad, but I didn't realize how bad. I think I always had a certain amount of faith in myself and plastic. A card in my wallet was a passport to the good life. I know I sound like some sort of cliché.

I am a cliché.

I went home and it was getting late, nine o'clock or so. Deidre was arranging a vase of flowers and there were tears in her eyes and Darin and Sarah were in the great room sprawled on the floor watching TV and the sound was turned up so high that cartoon laughter greeted me in the garage as soon as I stepped out of my car and there was no smugness that night as the garage door automatically shut.

"Your phone," Deidre said. "I tried to call you. Seventeen times I tried to call you."

And I was angry when I walked in the door. I was ready to yell at someone. I was ready to yell at the kids for something, anything, like leaving toys on the stairs or at Deidre for not vacuuming or something. I had to take my aggression out somehow and if my cards weren't all maxed out I would have gone down to Detroit and found a lap dance in some private room.

But I had to stay home.

"Yeah," I said, "I had it turned off. Sorry. I was golfing. I had money riding on each hole. I didn't want the phone to ring."

"Yeah… Money," she said. "That goddamn money."

And Deidre never swore, and certainly not in earshot of the kids.

I looked at her and I was ready to blow up. I was ready to fight but her tears and the flowers threw me off, probably because the combination of my sudden poverty and the flowers struck me as somewhat pathetic.

I took off my Nike golf hat and threw it on the counter after I shoved my clubs into the front hall closet and usually I took more care with them, especially my titanium driver.

"What's wrong?" I asked, with absolutely no compassion in my voice.

"What's wrong? What's *wrong*?" Deidre almost screamed and she hurled the vase of flowers at me and let me jump in here:

Neither one of us had physically abused the other up to this point. Sure I was a shitty husband and father, but I never raised my hand and we never really fought, if you can believe that. Our marriage was shallow, to be sure, too shallow for deep conversations or deep disagreements.

Until the money became a problem. That's what happens when a relationship is built upon a paper foundation, a foundation of money and stuff. The foundation can't stand any heat and it starts to burn.

And I watched it all burn down. I lit the match and poured starter fluid all over everything.

I dodged the flowers. They hit the kitchen wall right above my head and the water and bits of glass flew in the air and landed on my shoulders and head.

And the kids, they turned the TV up louder, not at all disturbed with the rage in the kitchen. I should have been bothered by that but I wasn't. I was too pissed off about maxed out credit cards and too distracted by Deidre's rage and tears.

Apparently, she went to the grocery store and all three of her credit cards were declined. She then started removing items one by one until she finally could use a card to pay for it. She apparently tried to buy two hundred bucks worth of groceries but wound up only being able to buy eighty dollars worth.

She still bought the flowers.

And she was mortified because the manager had to come over to the register and people in line behind her were getting angry, not to mention the neighbors and mothers from the school who recognized her.

"What the fuck?" I said to myself. I knew things were tough but I had always paid most of my bills so I wasn't quite sure what was going on. There was no reason for every card to be maxed out. I thought I was an organized executive type and I paid my bills and kept track of them on the computer.

I went to my home office, or den, or library, or whatever name you want to give to that extra room with French doors and a picture window.

I turned on the computer and sure enough, I had paid all the bills pretty much on time, or what I thought was on time, and I have to tell you something here about credit card companies.

They change their due dates.

For example, take your favorite credit card and let's say the bill is due on the fifteenth of every month. You make the payment automatically for a year and you start to do it without thinking and you mail it on the twelfth just to make sure it gets to that P.O. Box in the middle of nowhere on time. You want to make sure your check makes it to a small town in Iowa or Arizona or maybe Delaware or West Virginia.

Maybe even Arkansas.

And notice the bill never goes to where the banks are headquartered. Your check has no glamorous destination like New York City or Boston or even Chicago.

No. Louisville is about as hip as it gets.

And then, without warning you, the bank moves your due date to the tenth and you don't pay any attention and whammo, you're socked with late fees.

Late fees are a bitch. Twenty bucks here, thirty bucks there, and then sometimes they reduce your credit limit because you've been late too many times and then they start calling you and they had been calling me but I was never home.

And Deidre—the kids and groceries and other shopping kept her too distracted to give me any messages.

Anyway, I was late on a couple of the credit card bills but I'd been late before and it was no big deal.

But this time it was.

It was because I'd been bouncing checks and it took me a second to figure that out after I started checking all my accounts online.

The bank paid a lot of the checks anyway, but some they didn't.

They didn't pay my $1900 mortgage payment but they did honor the $400 check for Deidre's Chrysler Town and Country equipped with heated leather seats, a rearview camera and a DVD player and monitor for Darin and Sarah while they rode in the back.

For family trips, the salesman told Deidre and me when we signed the papers. But we never took family trips. The DVD player was used to quiet the kids on trips to the grocery store or school or the dentist's office or anywhere, really. The TV in the van was on as much as the TV was in the house, which was all of the time unless the kids were sleeping or no one was home.

That was paid, along with the payment on the Macy's account, which I was only paying the minimum on, and that was seventy-three dollars but the overdraft fees ate up what wasn't paid.

Even the $1900 for my mortgage. Yes, it is possible to fuck up your life very quickly.

How did I bounce so many checks? I'm sure you're saying to yourself that I must have been stupid and you would be right.

You could say irresponsible. You could even say immoral.

All of those would be right and if I were to ever go to trial I would say I was addicted, addicted to money, and Deidre was addicted to money and stuff and it's something like a drug. The credit card companies and banks and retailers and commercials on TV for financial planning and Viagra and resorts and automobiles are not much different than your street corner pusher passing out drugs to kids as they walk home from school.

Really.

Anyway, you know why I bounced so many checks so fast? I never really kept track of my money very well. It was just always kind of there. We had enough money to order pizza two nights a week and go out to eat three and I was often not around for any of those nights. We had enough money to make payments on the remodeled kitchen and the in-ground swimming pool along with car payments and mortgage payments and flowers every Tuesday and Saturday and a different arrangement would be there in the middle of the mahogany French Colonial dining room table that we never bothered to eat at.

So the bounced checks were bound to happen and I'm surprised that it took so long. I'm surprised that it didn't happen until 2005, late in the summer, my forty-something face starting to crease and fold and sag despite all the moisturizers and anti-wrinkle creams I rubbed into my face and I was planning on getting a facelift, maybe liposuction because of the love handles that were cascading over the waistband of my boxer shorts and the hair loss was starting to become difficult to mask.

I arranged and gelled my very thin hair every morning with no small measure of precision.

But all of that would have to wait.

That would all have to wait because I was broke. A loser. Up to my nose hairs in debt and I always knew I was in debt.

But I really didn't care until it came time to pay that restaurant bill.

Options.

I had to weigh my options.

But first I had to deal with my anger. I had to justify my anger. I had to blame somebody or someone for the bounced checks. I stared at the computer monitor and the electronic ledger for my checking account and my face got red and I started to grind my teeth and I remember hearing the cartoons blaring from the great room and the sound of Deidre sobbing from the kitchen as she swept the flower and vase debris from around the countertop island.

I was broke. Screwed. Fucked.

And I felt like a loser. I felt like someone had chopped my dick off with a machete and shoved it down my throat, as if to say a real man doesn't get himself in this predicament. A real man doesn't bounce checks and get in over his head. Someone on the upper floors of Midwestern doesn't go broke. Hell, an executive at

Midwestern plays golf every weekend *and* has a cottage on a lake in Northern Michigan *and* has enough money left over to invest in stock and mutual funds and have a good enough reason to watch the cable business channels.

I had none of those things.

I had a pool I was still paying for. A hot tub. An island in the center of the kitchen that at that moment was covered in rose petals and broken glass and water and probably part of my heart and soul. I had a wife who was a stay-at-home-lunatic mother. I had two kids who were automatons. I had a beer gut that was paid for with credit cards and I was paying for them still. I had a weakness for office girls and hookers and my orgasms with them left me feeling hollow and now as I look back almost dead.

I was a zombie in a Cadillac.

I needed money. I needed to get caught back up and I've seen the same commercials you've seen. I've seen the commercials with the poor slob pulling out the inside of his pockets to show their vacancy. I've seen the commercials with 1-800 numbers and web addresses that promise to make your red and miserable life black and blissful.

Money from your home now.

So that's what I did.

But I couldn't do anything until I found someone to blame.

None of this was my fault.

I blamed Deidre as I glared at the negative balance on my computer screen. She could have kept on working. She could have put the kids in daycare and gone back to Midwestern. She could have been on the third floor by now, I told myself. She could have been making forty grand a year or even more if she went up a couple of floors as an executive assistant. She could have worn skirts and heels every day like she used to instead of those designer sweat suits or black boots and jeans like all the other mothers crawling around the subdivision. If she was working we would have paid off the pool and the hot tub and maybe even the island in the kitchen.

Or we would have spent more.

So the blame.

I really couldn't blame Deidre, at least not for very long. I knew the kids were better off with their mother at home and all that other feel-good horseshit.

So I blamed the credit card companies. I blamed them for feeding me and I likened myself to a goldfish. I've heard a goldfish will eat and eat if you keep on feeding it and if you keep on feeding it eventually it will explode.

I saw myself, all of me, blood and guts and heart and soul, explode on the Swedish made desk in my office.

And that really sucked because the desk wasn't even paid for yet.

There I sat and I knew I couldn't blame Deidre and if I couldn't blame Deidre then I had to blame myself.

Blaming yourself takes a certain amount of responsibility.

And remember, responsibility can kill.

But I had to take some of the blame because I had always kept Deidre in the dark about our finances. I never discussed bank statements or credit card balances with her because if I did then she would have known what I was up to and I couldn't have that.

My financial habits were kept in the shadows.

And she didn't care. She had her cards and her van and the cards worked each time they were swiped and she was reasonably happy because her husband was making enough money to provide for her family and drown them in necessities and stuff.

Until that day at the grocery store.

Her shame and misfortune in front of the eyes of so many so-called friends or peers or people just like her was just too hard to take and the sting was even worse when Heather two doors down called just before I got home that day to see if "everything was all right" and Deidre had to lie, something about expired credit cards and grabbing the wrong purse.

Women never grab the wrong purse.

So I went back into the kitchen. Darin and Sarah were still on the floor watching cartoons in the great room. The sun was setting over the hedges and patio and hot tub, and the top of the pool was basking in a soft orange light and everything looked beautiful.

The blame and shame started building up in me and I had to do something with it. I ran out of my office and back to the kitchen.

I went to the sink and threw up.

"We have to cut back on things for a while," I said after I finished puking and I wiped my mouth with the back of my hand and I gave Deidre a brief explanation of our financial straits. I told her that all the cards were maxed out except for maybe the Sears card, which we used to buy washers and dryers and microwaves and sometimes clothes for the kids.

Deidre and I would never wear clothes from Sears.

I told her that things at work were slow and it was because of the economy and my monthly bonuses were smaller than they used to be. And that was only partly true. The economy in Michigan was and probably still is horrible. It will probably be horrible forever because of so many auto and manufacturing plants closing and moving overseas, and I remember how it was then, people leaving the state, houses not selling, and the office buildings surrounding Midwestern headquarters were half-empty, every building bearing For Lease and Space Available signs.

And Midwestern laid off people too, but not because we had to.

But because we could.

Every other company in the area was laying off workers and we found that to be a good corporate model. Just like General Motors, Ford, Chrysler, Pfizer, you name it.

Pay people the same and make them do more.

I was no different. I used to have two assistants and then they reduced me to one and I did have a gnawing fear that I might be one of the ones to be cut, but that fear was short-lived.

Because I was and still am the biggest bastard that ever worked at Midwestern Accident and Life. I don't give a damn about anybody else. I've had women crying to me on the phone after people beneath me had already denied their claims but women don't always take no for an answer so it would be up to me to tell them no. And these women, I've heard from women crying and screaming and I've heard their teeth chatter because they were calling me from a cell phone in Minnesota and because their houses burned down they were forced to live in their cars with their miserable husbands and frozen and hungry babies and I would say:

"Sorry, your policy clearly states you can't smoke in the house if you have a fireplace."

The bosses love me because I save them money. The lawyers love me because angry customers always threaten to sue and corporate lawyers love the smell of blood and they like to never lose.

So, my job was safe. It was safe even though I had to start sending my own faxes. I had to make my own appointments and spreadsheets.

And the layoffs would eventually mean bigger bonuses for me, but those would come too soon too late. The big bonus came after the fire and at that point I didn't need so much money anymore.

So I told Deidre we would have to live without some things for a while. We would have to not shop until I got paid, which was another week away unless I could figure something out.

"Not shop?"

"Right."

"What about food?"

"Nothing. We'll have to eat what's in the house."

"But we have no food here…"

And she leaned against the island, the track lighting reflecting off the hanging pots and pans making it look like there were two dozen shining and silvery suns above her head. Her mascara started to run and I said:

"We have a lot of food."

And I knew this to be true because the pantry was full of canned foods that I knew she bought because they were on sale. Organic chili. Franks and beans. SpaghettiOs. Canned salmon and tuna and chicken. There were boxes of cake mix, pancake and waffle mixes along with every imaginable canned vegetable.

Corn, sweet potatoes, squash, peas and beans, carrots.

A starving family of four in Africa could live for a year off of what we had in the pantry.

I opened the pantry and pointed inside. "We'll have to eat these," and I pulled out a bag of marshmallows with just a hint of dust on the packaging.

"Or this," I said as I showed her a can of low-sodium beef broth.

"Food," she said. "That's not food."

"It's going to have to be until I figure things out. We're just going to have to live a little simpler until things get back to normal. The economy will turn around. Things can't stay down forever.

"Maybe you should get a job," I said, and that was meant to deflect some of the responsibility for our misfortune away from me and onto her.

She walked away and went into the great room and collapsed on the couch and grabbed a parenting magazine as Darin and Sarah were still on the floor lying on their stomachs with their legs bent and their stocking feet hanging listlessly in the air. I grabbed that bag of marshmallows and a bottle of Heineken and went back to the computer and filled out applications for debt consolidation loans and mortgages and thought about what I would say to Reece back at the office on Monday and I knew I wouldn't go to Starbucks that morning just in case Reece was in line, and I thought that I probably wouldn't be going to Starbucks at all anymore.

There was no problem getting a loan to pay off some of our debt. I got one of those adjustable rate mortgages with a fixed rate for the first year. I went with an online bank out of Oklahoma and I was shocked when I saw how steep my debt actually was. I had never really thought about it before because my debt was nothing more than a series of monthly bills.

I was into credit cards for something like ninety thousand dollars.

But luckily, I had that much equity in my house. I was able to refinance and wrap that debt into a new mortgage, which meant I was back to square one on a thirty-year mortgage and instead of costing me $1900 a month my mortgage would cost $2299 and on paper a $2299 a month mortgage is no sweat for someone with my income.

Some cards were paid off; new cards came in the mail. Deidre went back to the grocery store and took up yoga to deal with her newfound financial stress even though she didn't really know the depth of our burden.

The incident at the grocery store had scarred her emotionally for life, so much so that our infrequent sex life quickly became dead. She fell in love with yoga and you would be surprised how much yoga costs. Classes and mats. Clothes and books.

I started golfing and going to strip clubs again along with renting the occasional hooker and I didn't care that they found me loathsome (I found myself sort of loathsome) but I didn't go at it with the same vigor.

It seemed as if the rented sex came with twenty-eight percent interest plus the transaction fee for a cash advance on my credit card.

Darin and Sarah went to school and were average. They received average grades and wore average clothes and our income stayed average for our neighborhood but things were starting to change.

Houses were being put up for sale and no one was buying them but I really didn't care for about a year. I had no problem making my $2299 a month payment, along with my new credit card and lease payments, and we did make some sacrifices.

We dropped the movie channels from our cable TV package. I bought beer in cans instead of bottles. Deidre stopped buying flowers every time she went to the grocery store.

She bought them every other time instead.

A year passed. Things went on as they had gone before and that tragic September Saturday was almost forgotten except for Deidre still cringed every time a credit card was swiped.

I told her not to worry. Everything was under control. I told her work was good, business was booming, and even with the rise in natural disasters, Midwestern was still holding its own.

But not really.

There were more layoffs and I was pressured to produce even more, to squeeze more pennies out of denied claims than ever before. I had to be more heartless and more ruthless and that was easy enough because I was trained to look at the paying of claims a certain way early on. The company reinforced that training each time I ascended a floor.

"Insurance is only peace of mind," they told me. "That's our business—peace of mind. We only exist to let our customers think they have all their bases covered and that way they can truly live. What middle-aged man doesn't start to think about leaving his wife behind? And he doesn't want to leave her behind empty-handed and he doesn't want to spend the last third of his life worrying about her. That's where we come in. We're here to take care of the living customer, not the beneficiary of a policy. Nor do we exist to rebuild a ruined house or repair a wrecked automobile. We do when we have to, of course, and that's where you come in…"

And you're probably wondering why I was so heartless and I could tell you that it was because the more claims denied the bigger my bonuses were and are and any reasonable red-blooded American company man will understand that.

There is no room for altruism in business. Altruism is something you learn about in high school and college and then you never think about it again.

But my heartlessness ran deeper than dollars and cents, and I will show you how deep in due time.

But back to 2005 and 2006.

I paid my new mortgage every month without a hiccup though in the spring I did get an advance on my 401(k) because the minimum monthly payments on my new cards were starting to get a little too steep. The 401(k) loan application raised eyebrows in the human resources department.

Someone in my position, someone above the fourth floor, should never have to get a 401(k) loan. I remember walking into a morning meeting a little bit late and the room grew quiet as soon as I walked in and everyone nodded to me except for Reece. He stared at his lap and sipped his Starbucks without acknowledging me at all.

The 401(k) loan kept me living the way I was used to living. I kept on spending money and then without warning my adjustable rate mortgage adjusted.

It went from $2299 to $2599 and that was enough to throw everything into chaos.

And that's what started my war.

You could call it a heartless war.

War is hell.

Hell is fire and misery.

First off, I called the Oklahoma mortgage company to see what the heck was going on.

I had forgotten I signed an adjustable mortgage or maybe the word adjustable meant nothing to me.

The company was gone, out of business. Their website wasn't functioning and that's all there was to it. My mortgage had been sold off by them several months prior. They sold it to a famous bank. Think a big bank but I won't name any names.

Think Chase. Think Wells Fargo. Think Bank of America. You get the picture.

I called the bank that held my mortgage and my call went to a phone bank in India.

"I can't afford this," I said.

"I understand."

"What can I do?"

"Get another mortgage. Would you like to talk to one of our mortgage specialists?"

I hung up.

I knew in an instant that I was at the bottom of a slippery slope. I knew then that it wouldn't matter if I refinanced every other day and took out loans, I would never get out the financial hole I was in. It was as if the slope was built out of shit, and the banks and credit card companies were standing on top of the hill throwing handfuls of shit at me as I kept on trying to climb out of debt.

You will say this was all my doing. You will say this is all self-inflicted. You will say that I put my signature on every credit and loan application. You will say that it was me who was living beyond my means.

But think about it. Am I the only one?

No. Of course not. Did your parents and grandparents live beyond their means back in the earlier part of the Twentieth Century, back in the days of Diners Club and American Express and little else?

No. They would have if they could have, but there wasn't the credit industry that you now see flourishing all around you. There were no call centers in India calling you if you were past due.

People lived off their paychecks because there was no one willing to lend them money against future paychecks.

In my case money was leant to me against every paycheck that I would ever earn for the rest of my life. I figured out that if I just made the minimum payment on all my credit cards (and stopped using them completely) it would cost me two grand a month and I wouldn't be paid off until I was ninety-three.

And the rate change came just as the lease on my Cadillac had ended. As usual, I went over the allowable miles. In the past I would simply write a check to cover the difference or roll that fee into the next lease but this time I couldn't write a check and my credit rating made it tough to roll the extra mileage into another lease, a newer Cadillac, and I had my eye on a black CTS.

But my credit rating made the CTS impossible. I was forced to buy my white Seville. I was so tired of the white Seville.

It was starting to make me feel old, so old in fact I would get up in the middle of the night in those early days of my ballooned mortgage and shame in having to drive a three-year-old car and stare at my face in the mirror. I stared at my receding hairline. I stared at the bags under my pale blue eyes that looked cold if not dead. I stared at the web of wrinkles fanning from the corners of my eyes to my temples, the lines in my forehead that were starting to crease and fold and sag, and I realized I had an old man's face. My father's face, except I didn't have the broken veins in my nose or along the ridge of my cheekbones. I didn't have the scotch and gin reddened face like my father, as if he was radiating warmth and gentle heat like a cozy fireplace.

My face.

One morning, just after I cut a check on the computer for my first whopping mortgage payment, I stared at my face long and hard and I thought about crying because I also had both car payments due and a week didn't go buy without some credit card bill being due but the cards would have to wait at least until my next paycheck and so would gasoline and carwashes, so would donuts and newspapers on Saturday and Sunday mornings.

I just couldn't *not* make one of the car payments. Five hundred bucks for my Cadillac per my loan agreement and $400 for Deidre's Chrysler Town and Country.

Imagine my embarrassment if my Cadillac was repossessed from the Midwestern parking lot. Imagine Deidre. Imagine her waiting for the kids at school as she stands in front of the doors talking to the other mothers. Imagine the minivan being left running to keep it warm or cool depending on the season. Imagine pop music playing not too softly from the radio, something Top 40 and familiar depending on the year and then imagine some greasy and burly tattooed repo man coming to take the van away in front of god, the other mothers, and the entire school.

I had to make the car payments.

I stared at my face and it started to shift and blur as my eyes focused and unfocused and started to tear. I saw my cheeks turning red and I encouraged that redness as I tried to make myself look more like my father.

The redness grew.

It crept down my neck and around my mouth and up to my forehead and the longer I stared the brighter it became and soon my face started to glow. Like burning coals; like metal glowing and hot, waiting to be forged by a blacksmith's hammer.

Fire.

And I'm not one to be metaphysical, much less spiritual, but something stirred inside my soul the moment my face started to catch on fire. I felt right. I felt at peace. I felt like I belonged in flames. Something like hell, maybe, I don't know. But it felt right and I felt calm, calmer than I had felt in a long, long time.

But the calmness was short-lived. I had stared in the mirror while the shower was running and steam filled the bathroom and finally it covered the mirror and the flame was dimmed in waves of steam that looked like so much smoke and I turned away just as the last bit of fire glowed from the mirror.

And then an idea struck. I felt confident, invigorated. I felt as if everything was going to be okay.

Time. I just needed a little time to put everything together and then my financial troubles would be solved.

But I didn't have a lot of time because that month was the month from hell.

I made the car and mortgage payments and I decided to be responsible and call the credit card companies I was choosing to ignore. There was the Chase Visa, the Wells Fargo MasterCard. Macy's, Home Depot; all of them weren't getting paid that month.

But I called. I explained to them my situation. I said I was short on funds (no shit) and I lied a little bit. I said there was a death in the family. I said I had to bury a relative and fly out of state and pay for the funeral and they bought it and offered their condolences but in the same breath they said I still had to pay them and I said, oh yeah, of course.

And I think those breaths were taken in India and I don't want to beat a dead horse here but the banks and credit card companies make a huge profit off of you going to the mall buying scented candles and purses and pocket watches. You would think the people fighting in their trenches would speak with an accent you can understand.

I said next month. I will catch up next month and I might even pay you off next month because there's a will hanging in the balance and I should be a huge beneficiary.

Oh, okay, they said, well thank you for your business Mr. Dash but it doesn't sound that way coming out of their Indian mouths and I have nothing against Indians but I feel a little uncomfortable pouring my heart out and confessing my financial trespasses to someone living in a third-world country where I've heard shit and piss flow down every street.

And back in the States, I later learned, the credit card companies don't want you to *ever* pay them off. They need you to pay the bare minimum because that's where the money is, on you paying five hundred dollars a month on a ten-thousand-dollar balance and that five hundred bucks goes mainly to the interest so it will take you a hundred years to pay off that ten thousand bucks. And they're banking on you not being able to pay more than the minimum payment. They know you'll pay the bill and charge your groceries later because you've used up your cash making payments on cell phones and cable TV.

They've got you. They've got you by the balls and you put your balls in their hands.

Maybe because they made your balls feels so good. I don't know.

But I had a plan. Fire and smoke. And I was going to pay them within the next couple of months. All of them.

And it wouldn't cost me a thing.

Except for maybe my soul and all that comes with it.

But I had sold my soul long before that. A man that can do what I've done cannot have a soul or whatever you call that innate sense of right or wrong.

Call it a conscience or a heart.

Have you ever wondered about the true nature of good and evil? Have you ever wondered about heaven and hell and the hand of God and the work of the Devil?

I don't have to wonder about it.

I know it.

I know I'm no good. I know my soul was torched and burned while sitting at my father's feet as he drank his gin and tonic and talked about money and policies with my uncles as they sat in our back yard for some barbecue.

"A man can't say he's lived his life unless he's made some kind of mark," my father would say and my uncles would agree.

"You've got to get what you can from this life. You have to be able to enjoy life," and then my father pointed with his finger to where in the yard our swimming pool was going to go, along with the Florida room and he talked about the leather of his Lincoln and how a Cadillac just can't compare even though he thought about driving one but the test drive at the dealership proved his point that a Lincoln is the only way to go.

Back to my plan to pay off my debt in a month.

A Monday in February, 2007. That's right. I lose track but 2007 was when the bottom fell and the rates adjusted and the whole state was sweating recession. Business was slow and I wandered around the lower floors and the banks of office girls and clerical boys sat upright as I walked amongst their ranks.

I was the notorious hatchet man. I was the guy who was sent to lay people off and the one to deny claims, the dark prince of the upper floors.

I walked around with my suit jacket off and my sleeves rolled up and my tie loosened. I tried to look comfortable, friendly not intimidating, even though I loved the asshole image I portrayed.

Think about it. Assholes at your work are always treated with respect in person even though they are spat upon verbally when they're not around.

I found a corner of the fourth floor, an area designated for the group that types up the policies for the newest and the high-risk clients.

"Hi," I said to a mousy looking girl with glasses and a vaguely hairy upper lip and I still leered at her because she was wearing a short skirt and the legs were shapeless but long and thin.

She looked up from her monitor surrounded by stuffed animals and coffee mugs full of pens and phrases and I saw the flash of fear in her eyes when she recognized Chas Dash.

She cleared her throat and said something like, "Sir?"

"I need you to print me all the credit reports of all the high-risk clients from the last month," I told her. "I'm working on a new project and you can't tell *anyone*." I leaned in to her. "It's from the fourteenth floor. You know, we're not sure what kind of rates and coverage we really want to offer all of these people. It's stuff for the actuaries to sort through, but I've got a nose for risk and reward.

"In fact, meet me at lunch at Bennigan's. Not the one at the mall near the office but the one down the road a few miles. Bring the credit reports, but limit it to those who live in this part of Oakland County. It's easier to focus our study on one demographic. One o'clock. That should give you enough time. I'll buy."

I got to Bennigan's a half hour early. The inside was dim lights and pop music and I sat at the bar and drained two scotch and sodas as I said a prayer to the credit card gods to make sure I'd have enough of a limit on one of my cards to pay for my drinks and her meal.

She showed up, Stephanie or Tiffany, I don't remember her name exactly. I remember her clunky glasses, her slightly kinky and pinned-up hair. I remember the tight maroon sweater over her nearly flat chest and her short skirt and stockings hugging a narrow waist and thin, long legs.

We took a booth in the corner of the restaurant. She gave me two manila envelopes bursting at the seams. I signaled the waitress and got another scotch and soda and what's-her-face ordered some kind of salad with low-fat dressing.

She ate and tried to talk and I could tell she was nervous but I ignored her. I was reading the credit reports: suburbanites with credit scores in the four and five hundreds paying for life insurance because their prime had passed them.

Million-dollar policies for eighty-nine bucks a month, insurance so their middle-aged wives can pay everything off when they croak and maybe bury them too.

Some scores were even lower, some a little higher and I could tell by the addresses which of the new customers were upper-middle-class slobs like me, overextended schmucks with lives filled with crap and unrealized desire.

The bill came. I told Tiffany or Melanie to go back to work and I thanked her and I told her to keep her mouth shut and I was nice about it. If I wasn't so distracted with credit reports, my impending financial doom, and my grand plans, I would have been nicer, flirty maybe.

I would have tried to have a go at her. I didn't see a wedding ring on her finger.

But I was off my game. My mind was filled with fire and revenge and sex was the last thing on my mind.

I didn't know it at that point, but I wouldn't be playing the game ever again, at least not the same way.

I took the reports home and sat at my desk. I selected three customers who lived nearby but not close enough to raise any suspicion. They lived like two suburbs over and you'd have to look at a map of the northern suburbs of Detroit, communities laid out like squares and grids. Boxes of congestion and subdivisions and highways and office buildings.

And make that half-empty office buildings as of late along with houses for sale that no one wanted to buy and I had thought about selling my house but the market started to fade just after I refinanced and that meant there was absolutely no way I could sell it for what I owed on it.

I was stuck because my mortgage was upside down.

But I wasn't worried. My plan should and had to work.

It was easy. I was going to rob those three houses.

I chose those three because their houses were worth the most and the inhabitants had tremendous debt, debt in six figures, even exceeding my debt. One house belonged to a school superintendent and the other two belonged to men who owned their own automotive supply companies and I could tell in an instant that their companies were probably booming in the Nineties but dying in the Two Thousand and Zeroes.

I was going to break in during the night while they were sleeping (I wasn't worried about alarms because the alarm companies reported their delinquencies and it looked like their alarms had long been turned off) and I wasn't going to steal much, maybe some jewelry or paintings or something. No stereos or TVs.

I would be driving a Cadillac, after all, not exactly your average bad-guy-panel-truck-getaway-car.

And you're probably wondering why I would break in if somebody was home, even if they were sleeping.

Because I didn't care if I got caught.

That and I knew I wouldn't get caught.

The execution of my plan. The first house, the first target, the first victim and casualty.

The first battle.

Picture a crisp winter night. Picture twinkling stars and a full moon and freshly fallen snow that is white and twinkling except for the snow that lies along the boulevards and main roads.

That snow is blackened with exhaust.

It's about two in the morning. I had been sleeping on the couch in front of the TV. I had started doing that immediately after the plan came to my head because I didn't want Deidre to hear me sneaking out at night. She didn't even question my not sleeping with her.

People who barely talk really don't need to sleep together.

Two in the morning.

I had parked my car on the street the evening before because I didn't want anyone in my family to hear the motor and rattle of the garage door opening. I didn't want them to hear the Cadillac ignite even though an eight-cylinder Cadillac is pretty damn quiet. I wore a jogging suit on top of an ancient set of long underwear that was so tight it was riding up my ass and suffocating my balls. My stomach stretched the zipper into a sort of arc shaped like the trajectory of a perfectly driven golf ball and my weapon, an imitation Glock from Argentina that I bought years ago when I first started driving into the city for recreational purposes, didn't move at all as I had tucked it into the waistband just a tad to the left of my crotch.

And bullets. I had real bullets in the gun this time. Before, I had just used it as a prop in my glove box, keeping it there for security and comfort and nothing else.

Just like life insurance.

I planned on having to use it on this night.

I drove to the next town to the north, the next square-shaped community, and found my target, a large house, four thousand square feet, in a subdivision full of towering four-thousand-square-foot houses that were identical save different colored bricks.

I had spent the past two evenings casing the house, driving around the subdivision, and no one seemed to notice me. All the houses were shut up tight and I could see occasional shadows and figures behind open drapes and closed blinds and besides, a Cadillac didn't look exactly out of place.

The house seemed to be inhabited by a middle-aged couple. Their credit report was a wreck. The house had been refinanced a million times and each one of their cards was maxed out and they had every card you could think of, even Diners Club.

And I thought I was bad.

He was past due on his lease payment for a Lincoln Navigator. She was a little more practical. She leased a Volkswagen Passat. The payments were mostly on time.

He came home late both nights I watched and I had to guess he was coming home from some second job because he was a school administrator during the day. She was already home because I could see the VW in the garage as it opened to accommodate his Lincoln. I couldn't catch a glimpse of him and I kind of wanted to know if he was big or small just in case I had to confront him physically because I have never been much of a fighter and I was starting to get a little nervous about my whole plan.

But desperation makes you do crazy things and sometimes fear and reason go out the window.

Wait a minute. Let me take that back. I have to clear something up and maybe this will make sense to you later on. I've always known right from wrong. I knew my plan was and is illegal, immoral, repulsive. Hideous. Gruesome. I know.

It's not desperation that makes you do crazy things.

Maybe it's preservation.

Preservation and revenge.

I sat in my car and watched the house after the gentleman returned home.

He had a name but it escapes me now.

When someone comes home you expect a series of lights to turn on, one by the side door that leads into the kitchen, and then maybe one in the living room or family room.

But this house had nothing. No lights. The school administrator entered from the garage and the house remained dark as if it was vacant. The wife was sitting around in the dark before the husband came home and he found his way in the dark also.

I thought it was odd, so on the second night, just after eleven, I parked the Cadillac halfway down the block and walked around the house and in the back I saw the glow of a TV's shifting light from the second-story window.

Four thousand square feet and they were living in the three hundred square feet of their bedroom, or so it seemed.

So I knew what I would do.

I would be armed with my gun, a lighter, a dishtowel, gloves, a can of lighter fluid and a bag to carry whatever it was I was going to steal.

Except the whole idea behind my plan wasn't really contingent on stealing my way to financial solvency.

The solvency would come later.

I would break the back window in the kitchen, the one through the sliding door that led to the deck full of new lawn furniture. I would break it with the towel wrapped around the handle of the gun and the noise would hopefully be deafened enough so it wouldn't rise above the sound of the upstairs television.

But I wanted to be heard, just not in a jarring way.

I would walk through the kitchen, open drawers and strew things about, make it look like someone was stealing and if I had the presence of mind I would take the phone off the hook if one was still in the kitchen in this age of pervasive cell phone use.

There was a phone in the kitchen.

I did all of those things and my heart was racing and I felt it pound in my ribcage and I could hear the sound of my pumping blood echo in my ears as if someone was pressing the same low note piano key over and over but in double time and it was hard to make the kitchen look like a mess because it already was one. There was a pile of dishes in the sink just as there was trash cluttering the countertops and spilling out of the trash can and onto the floor. The stench was overpowering, and I could see discarded banana peels, cheese slice wrappers and pizza boxes as soon as my eyes adjusted to the light.

I could also hear the drone of flies above my beating heart.

I found the phone easily enough. I took it off the hook and then I started up the stairs and the staircase proved no different than the kitchen; there were unopened bills and letters and dirty clothes along the whole of the staircase and it was all I could do not to trip as I drew my gun and it was at this point I expected some sort of confrontation. I expected the guy to come at me with a baseball bat or even some kind of weapon.

But no.

My march up the stairs and through the darkened and cluttered upstairs hallway was unimpeded.

I stopped at the top of the stairs. The gun in my right hand pointed in the darkness in front of me and my hand was far from steady.

I stepped forward slowly, deliberately, my heart racing, my breath hyperventilating, and I thought about turning back for a moment. About running back through the broken sliding door and through the snow and the crystal night back to my Cadillac and the seats would be leather and heated and they would cradle and comfort me back home to Deidre and the kids and maybe I would kiss Deidre softly and climb into bed with her and I would start to have sex with her and it would be the first time we made love in weeks if not months.

I guess you could call it making love or you could call it getting off.

But I didn't turn back. I thought about the bills hanging over my head. I thought about the embarrassing episodes and my life slipping away and I feared losing the house and being forced to live in some cramped apartment, my Cadillac parked in some carport among Malibus and Hyundais.

I kept going. All the bedroom doors were closed and I spied a shifting light underneath one at the end of the hall.

The master bedroom.

I debated about how I would enter the room, whether I would quietly open the door and tiptoe in or just kick it open like Chuck Norris.

I don't remember how I came to the decision, but it came quickly.

I strolled in rather casually, as if I were entering my own bedroom at home. I almost could have been whistling except I had my gun drawn as I entered. I had my gun drawn as I swung my body and extended arm and faced the school man and his wife lying in the light of the muted and moving TV.

Now, you would think someone would react to a stranger barging into their bedroom in the middle of the night and they did know I was there, both of them did. Their eyes followed me as I approached the bed. I'm guessing they woke up when I swung the door open and caused the knob to bounce on the adjacent wall or even while I was stumbling through their cluttered kitchen.

I saw their eyes open, both of them, man and wife lying on their backs in an oversized bed with an opulent headboard behind them. I was expecting them to jump up and scream, but no, they stared at me from across the cluttered bedroom that had several weeks of dirty clothes thrown about the floor and I could even smell hints of body odor mixed with the scent of urine and perfume and aftershave.

My heart, it stopped and started and everything seemed to move in slow motion as I walked to the bed and approached the prone couple and it was like they were already dead except for the darting of their eyes.

They watched me with the gun and neither moved a muscle. There wasn't even a twitching of neck or facial muscles and there was no fear in their eyes.

Only resignation.

Only acceptance.

I stood at the foot of the bed and fired and said:

"Take that."

I thought about the toothless dude who sold me the gun from the trunk of a 1984 Chevy Caprice in Detroit. He told me about the merits of the gun I chose. He told me about accuracy and stopping power.

The gun fired. A flash in the dark. A recoil against my arm and shoulder and a bullet in each forehead.

The holes in the forehead weren't clean little circles like I imagined. There was a mess, a collage of blood and skin and bone and hair splattered against the pillows and headboard.

And still, the eyes remained open and mostly unchanged.

Their eyes weren't any deader than they were before I fired my gun.

My beating heart slowed. I took a deep breath and started rifling through drawers.

I had to make it look like a burglary. I had to actually steal something.

I had no idea what burglars were supposed to steal.

I found the man's wallet on the nightstand. I opened it up: stacks of credit cards and two one-dollar bills.

I took the money and threw the credit cards into the air.

I found a small jewelry box on the vanity. Rings and earrings and necklaces and I have no idea if any of them were worth anything. I took them all, stuffing them into my little plastic shopping bag.

I then poured starting fluid on some of the clothes and magazines on the bedroom floor and lit them. They ignited quickly and surely and flames rose ankle high and I left the room and went through some of the spare bedrooms that were equally disheveled except for one that appeared to be a child's room and it was neat and tidy but it smelled like mold and dust and I had to think it belonged to a now-dead child and it remained just so because it was some sort of shrine.

I tore that room up too, tried to find something of value but there was only socks and underwear meant for a small boy and baseball cards.

I kept a handful of the baseball cards because you just never know.

I went back downstairs, poured starter fluid on the couch and kitchen floor and turned all the stove burners on high.

A gas stove.

I lit some of their unopened bills: Chase, Macy's, Marathon, Countrywide, Detroit Edison, Verizon Wireless, Comcast, AT&T.

I lit them, dropped them on the kitchen floor, and said:

"Take that."

I went out the kitchen door and walked out the patio and I was glad it was shoveled because I didn't want to leave any boot prints.

I ran to my car.

I heard about the explosion the next morning on the radio as I drove to work.

I said:

"Take that."

So, you're probably wondering why someone had to die just so I could steal a handful of what was nothing more than not-so-precious jewelry and two dollars.

You're probably wondering why I didn't flinch as I saw two innocent people die by my soft hands.

Well, I'll tell you.

My reasons were twofold. First and foremost it was the first step in my plan to become debt-free and I will explain how that worked out later and it only worked because I got lucky but it came with a substantial cost.

And secondly I was at war. The couple I killed was deep in debt. Deeper than me, probably about a hundred thousand in the hole and that didn't include mortgages or car payments and if they were dead no one could collect. If they were dead the banks would have to go after their house but if their house was torched then it would be tough.

Take that.

And again, you could say it was that couple's fault for getting in too deep but again I say aren't the drug pushers punished by law just as much as the drug users?

Explain the difference to me. Go ahead, try, and guess what?

You can't.

Except in this case the pushers are legal corporations with tons of political clout and laws protecting their practice of usury, which the bible said was a sin.

Or so I've heard. I've never really read the bible.

So the couple dead in their bed surrounded by a ring of fire were a casualty, collateral damage, and you would be hard pressed to convince me that I didn't do them a favor. In fact, I think they didn't move when they saw me and my gun because they wanted to die. The fight and joy for life was taken out of them months or years ago by mounting bills and upper-middle-class poverty. They enjoyed a life of spend spend spend and it cost them in the end.

Take that, I said to myself as I hopped into the shower at about three that morning after peeling off my sweat suit, which was indeed soaked with sweat.

The sweat of adrenaline and indifference.

I washed the smell of gunpowder off of my fingers, I washed the smell of that house off of my body and off of my hair, and I rubbed my scalp fiercely as if that would take the recent memory away.

But the memory really didn't bother me. I felt vindicated, just, like a revolutionary taking a stand against tyranny.

My plan was starting off so nicely.

One battle down and I had two more planned in the immediate future and I wanted to have about six similar battles before the execution of my plan and I already had a map of metro Detroit marked with targets in my head.

I had targets in Birmingham, Grosse Pointe Woods and Shores, Plymouth, Rochester Hills.

I was going to do one or two a week and make it look like some sort of crime wave. The police would be looking for a petty criminal who robbed houses, murdered the inhabitants, and then set the place on fire.

And I also knew the police would find a common thread among the victims. I've watched enough TV over the years to figure that much out. I knew they would see that all the victims had policies at Midwestern and they would also maybe see they were deep in debt.

I had to make sure that no roads pointed to me and that meant I had to deal with Stephanie or Tiffany, the girl with the clunky glasses. If the police came sniffing around they would see a report with my victims was gathered and printed. They would see the computer login of the girl with the clunky glasses. They would come and talk to her. She would tell them about me even though she promised not to tell a soul.

This wouldn't do.

So the next day, after my first battle, I was tired. Damn tired. I got to the office at eight thirty and if I wasn't a broke ass I would have gone to Starbucks and got a double espresso or something loaded with caffeine to get me going but no, I was too poor for Starbucks and all my remaining credit cards were pretty much maxed out so I had to drink the office coffee instead and I shoveled down ten Styrofoam cups worth of the stuff before ten in the morning.

At ten fifteen I went to find Tiffany and you know what? She looked better. She got rid of the clunky glasses and cut her hair and had it straightened and I barely recognized her.

"Wow," I said to her and I meant it.

She blushed and smiled into her lap and said, "Hello, Mr. Dash."

I stood in front of her desk and stared at her for an instant and I might have been leering but thoughts of my plan interrupted that. I said goodbye and I walked away and I wanted to talk to her some more because hell, she looked all right but up close she wasn't great because she really could have used braces for at least her bottom row of teeth and a facial would have been a good idea to unclog her pores especially those in her forehead as I saw zits straining through her make-up.

I never would have let Deidre come to the office with zits on her forehead.

I went upstairs and didn't do much work that day. I surfed the internet and pretended to be busy. I went to lunch but just sat in my car because I didn't have any money and I pondered what to do about Tiffany.

And then it came to me as I saw Stephanie hop into her Ford Focus on her way out to lunch or wherever it is that semi-homely girls go during their break.

I went back to my desk and drank coffee and water to fill my stomach and I thought that maybe mild starvation would cause me to lose my paunch but all mild starvation did for me was give me dandruff and make my face crumble into some sort of ash and put bags under my eyes.

The paunch, it's still there.

But anyway, who really cares about my paunch? Take a look at me now and the last thing you would notice is my paunch.

I did some work that afternoon, stuff that I should have done that morning. The caffeine had me buzzing nicely and I almost forgot about my current situation for the odd moment here and there but the feelings of normalcy quickly passed as my mission loomed over me and darkened my mood like a total eclipse of the sun.

Four o'clock. I cleaned off my desk and logged off my computer and sat in my car with the key turned on but the engine off so I could listen to the radio and not waste any gas.

I listened to the Eighties station and felt almost young, singing along with the Thompson Twins.

Hold Me Now.

Deidre and I used to do it to Hold Me Now, but my thrusts were in a quicker time than the music. My thrusts were always urgent and furious.

Think Nirvana. Think Smells Like Teen Spirit.

I sat in my car and waited for Tiffany or Stephanie and I wasn't sure what time she would get out of work. The lower people sometimes left at five or even six depending on business but business was soft and she came walking out of the atrium at five o'clock sharp as the sun dropped behind the Midwestern building and shadows fell on everything.

I followed her Focus and I have to tell you it's very hard following someone in rush hour traffic, especially if that someone knows who you are.

You have to stay close behind them but not too close. You have to have a couple of car lengths in front of you but you can't be too far behind in case your quarry turns or changes lanes.

And in this case Tiffany quickly pulled on to the on-ramp for I-75 heading south.

I had to accelerate quickly and veer over two lanes to keep up with her and I found myself right behind her as she merged into the freeway traffic and I thought for sure she would be able to spot me but I had the dying sun and headlights on my side and it quickly became dark enough to hide the facial features of every driver on the road and I started to relax as Tiffany's little Focus meandered down the pot-holed freeway and I was surprised at how far she lived from the office.

Clear on the other side of Detroit. Past downtown and south of the city in the working-class Downriver area.

I always thought she was a homebody type, not one to work far from where she lived.

She lived in Southgate, a pretty bland city full of small single-family homes, shopping centers and apartment blocks.

She pulled into her apartment, a drab looking building of empty balconies and older cars.

She parked right by her door on the lower level and I parked on the far side of the lot next to the dumpsters and I don't think she noticed me and there I sat as I watched her walk in.

I sat and waited.

I waited to see if anyone else approached her apartment, someone like a roommate or a boyfriend. I watched her lone window with its closed curtains backlit by some dim lamp. I was looking for shadows of more than one person but there was just Stephanie, her silhouette recognizable in the early evening gloom.

I drove away and parked in front of a small strip mall half a block away. I took note of the stores—an adult video store, a smoke shop, and a payday advance place and I looked long and hard at the payday advance place because a few bucks in my hand would have felt all right.

But I didn't go in. I couldn't let the world know I was in Southgate that night.

I walked to Tiffany's apartment on a crumbling sidewalk along a busy road whose name I really didn't know. Later, after it was all over, I would get lost in her neighborhood while trying to find I-75 North.

I knocked on her door and I thought I should be nervous. I thought my heart would be pounding through my chest and I thought there would be sweat pouring out of my armpits and temples.

But no. I was calm and cool and a little aroused even when Tiffany opened the door and squinted at me in the dark.

"Mr. Dash?"

"Yeah, but please, call me Chip. I'm sorry to bother you like this, but I had to see you," and I stuck my head in the door to make sure she was alone. The apartment was clean and small and decidedly empty and quiet. The television wasn't even on and I was certain she lived alone.

Which she did.

She gave me a nervous smile and she was still in the same skirt she wore at work except now her blouse was untucked and she had pulled her shoes and pantyhose off. She was walking around barefoot and I stared at her feet.

Feet. I liked her feet.

"Can I come in?"

Reluctantly, she let me in.

I was going to make small talk. I was going to tell her that I was in love with her and had been dying to see her, but I didn't bother with small talk.

As soon as she closed the door behind me I grabbed her neck and started squeezing and she tried to scream and wriggle free but she was too small and too surprised to do anything.

She passed out after about ninety seconds and I kept on squeezing well past that even though my hands and wrists were burning from exertion but I had to make sure she was dead and when I was sure she was good and dead I dropped her on her couch and it was then I noticed that she had a cat who was curled up on the back of the couch staring at me with a knowing look.

I put her on the couch and stared at her for a second because her skirt had been hiked up during the struggle and I was surprised to see that she was wearing thong underwear.

I shrugged my shoulders and I told myself that I could never look a gift horse in the mouth.

I pulled down her underwear and pulled down my pants and I went at it like an eighteen-year-old in the back seat of a car.

When I was done I zipped up my pants and pulled the batteries out of the smoke detector on the wall. I poured some lighter fluid on Stephanie and dropped a match and left. I checked the windows of the rest of the apartment building as I walked away and wouldn't you know that every shade was drawn and every door was shut and probably locked.

Now, you're probably wondering at what point did I go from suburban family guy to cold-blooded killer and necrophiliac?

The point is there was no point.

I had been and always will be the same kind of person. I've gone to church and prayed to Jesus and it's not like I don't believe in any of that stuff. It's not that I don't believe that someday, maybe, I'll go to hell and burn for my sins.

But ask yourself what you would do if you were in the same situation as me. Would you roll over and surrender and let the banks repossess your life? Would you live on the street and walk around like a bum and dig through dumpsters looking for change and food?

Or would you fight? Would you strike back at those who wronged you, at those who fucked you with their might and interest rates?

You're damn right you would fight. You just might not be as vicious as me.

I guess it all depends on how you want to live your life.

Tiffany's death made the news. There was a mention of rape and arson. I guess the apartment burned pretty good before any of the neighbors noticed and called the fire department.

I still don't know what happened to the cat.

There was no mention that it was connected to the first house I hit and I knew there wouldn't be. I didn't rape anyone that first time. There was a plea from the Southgate police along with a number for the Wayne County Sheriff's office in case anyone knew what happened to Stephanie because her death was a mystery and there were interviews with her mother crying in front of the TV cameras and you would think this would have made me feel bad at least a little bit.

But it didn't.

Tiffany was collateral damage.

The police came to the office and fanned out across the lower floors, asking co-workers if they knew of a boyfriend that might have been angry or even a fellow worker who might have been stalking her.

No, they all said, she kept to herself, she talked about her family and cat all the time…

The police didn't even make it past the tenth floor. They didn't bother with those of us who had an eagle eye view of the parking lot and bands of asphalt that swirled around the office. That's how it always is; people in power are seldom accused or suspected of anything.

The police came and went and that was it. I knew they would have samples of my DNA and that was fine. My blood and fingerprints had never been part of a larger database and my DNA would only tell the police that I was just another forty-something suburban white male, just one in a million in metropolitan Detroit.

Good luck finding that guy.

My plan was to hit a house every week but not on the same day. I didn't want to give the police too much of a pattern to follow.

I didn't want Friday night to be cat burglar-arsonist night.

I had a rough sketch in my brain and my next target was one in Grosse Pointe, just off Jefferson Avenue near the Detroit border.

I could do my thing and disappear in the city and no one would come chasing after me. Detroit is something like the Wild West and I hear the mayor and police are all corrupt, giving it that lawless atmosphere.

At least in my opinion.

But I'm not interested in the problems of Detroit or any other social problems. I have problems of my own, not as bad now, but the war wages on.

I could so easily make forays into Detroit, but let's face it, a bank won't miss someone earning and owing five and four figures a year.

Nope. They won't miss them at all. Someone who is broke because they are in debt five or eight thousand dollars is nothing.

The bigger prizes are in the sprawling houses that you see in far flung suburbs or the BMW driving executive in a trendy urban neighborhood.

They are the ones who make six figures and owe every bit of that and pay and pay each month.

Those are the prizes. Those are the best targets, generally speaking.

And I do use a lot of generalizations but that's what our country and the world has become.

We are demographics and numbers. We are tax brackets and race. We are zip codes and gender.

We are statistics. Bars on a graph.

Generalizations.

The house in Grosse Pointe was just like the first one in Rochester Hills except it was older, probably built in the Twenties with now faded red brick, small paned windows, and a large wooden front door. The neighborhood certainly had charm with its old-fashioned streetlights and towering ancient trees, as if the neighborhood had a soul unlike my own neighborhood and the one in Rochester full of shiny new houses and pretty people.

But the neighborhood didn't matter; the only thing that mattered was the occupants of the house.

They were the same sort of occupants as the one in Rochester, a middle-aged couple, late forties, early fifties, and they had stuff, you know, new cars in the garage, a second mortgage on a cottage on a lake in Northern Michigan that was going into foreclosure, and tons of crap inside their house.

Their house was full of crap as I broke a window in the dining room at one in the morning. I waded through crap and knick-knacks that surrounded their antique looking furniture that was meant to go with their antique house.

At least that's what I thought I saw through the moonlight that poured through the small lead windows.

And this time I got confronted.

As soon as I crashed onto the dining room floor I heard a rustling from upstairs and the pounding of feet coming down the stairs. I drew my gun and saw a stocky figure standing in front of me as soon as my eyes focused. I saw a short fat arm pointed at me and I saw the silhouette of a snub-nosed revolver pointed at me.

This guy owned his own company and was probably a son-of-a-bitch. Most bosses are. You already know that.

I fired. I fired first and last and the figure stumbled backward and I heard a feminine scream from the second floor and without thinking I flew up the wide and ornate staircase and followed the light emitting from a solitary lamp in what proved to be the master bedroom.

I tore into the bedroom and saw a shivering middle-aged female figure underneath the sheets of a four-post king-sized bed that required a small step to climb into.

I fired into the quivering form.

One two three shots and the form stopped shaking.

"Take that," I said and I poured starting fluid on the bed and lit it on fire and I rummaged through the also very cluttered room quickly, yanking jewelry from old jewelry boxes on top of the dresser and vanity and there was a fair amount of jewelry and I stuffed into my pockets causing them to bulge and my sweatpants might have been pulled down because of the weight if they weren't so tight.

I ran downstairs, poured fluid on the dead man lying on the dining room floor surrounded by stacks of magazines and newspapers and god-knows-what-else and my heart was barely beating, which I thought was odd because it started to race as soon as I heard the wail of sirens above the hiss of flames.

I gingerly climbed out the same broken window and ran through the back yard and over the fence and into the next block.

Sirens and flashing lights tore through the neighborhood and I stayed in the shadows until I got to my Cadillac parked half a mile away in the back of an upscale seafood restaurant on Mack Avenue that still appeared to be open.

No one saw me, at least not that I noticed, and I had camouflage in my favor as I drove away, just another white guy in a Cadillac driving through comfortable streets, past the speeding fire trucks and ambulances that were heading toward my recent target.

"Take that," I said as I found the expressway and headed back home.

I had won another battle and I was winning the war.

Chas Dash, 2. Bank of America, Chase, Wells Fargo, Countrywide, etc.... 0.

Now, the stuff I actually did steal became a minor problem. I was too afraid to take the stuff to a pawn shop because I was afraid the police might be keeping an eye on the pawnbrokers in light of the heinous burglaries.

Yes, they were heinous. War is heinous.

War is hell.

I couldn't leave it in plain sight in my house because Deidre would get suspicious, or at least question me about those recently acquired piles of jewelry that weren't bought for her and I didn't want to spin any more lies because I have to tell you I had gotten tired of lying all the time.

Lying is a pain in the ass because one lie leads to another lie and one can't help but to contradict oneself when the truth emerges.

For example, I once told Deidre a few years back that I went bowling when I actually went to a motel with an escort and when I called her from work the next day I told her my business meeting from the night before was a disaster and that I was sorry I didn't kiss her before I left for work that morning but I was too tired and depressed. I actually didn't kiss her because I was afraid she would smell the stale snatch on my breath, but that is another story.

"I thought you went bowling."

I paused.

"I did," I said, "but I only bowled one game because I had to meet some people at the airport *after*..."

And so the truth and lies went and I had gotten tired of it. And the War was my chance to clean the slate, to start over, to reinvent myself.

The War was my chance to make a difference in the world, to bring the banks to their knees or if not their knees then maybe punch them in the mouth. I thought that maybe once I got rolling I would send letters to the newspapers and banks themselves.

Forgive all debts or the deaths will continue... or something like that.

But those grand plans would and will have to wait for later.

I had to find a place to hide the loot.

And I really didn't have a place to hide it so I threw a lot of it away. I put it in my trash at the curb on a Tuesday morning, so many pearls and emeralds and diamonds mixed in with coffee grounds and tampon wrappers. Not to mention used tissue, leftover pizza. You name it.

I did give Deidre a diamond tennis bracelet that I took from the Grosse Pointe house.

She squealed with delight as I dropped it in her hand on a Wednesday evening after I got home from work.

On February 14th. Valentine's Day, to be exact.

"I thought we could talk about my sleeping on the couch," I said, as if marital discourse had forced me on the couch.

"Yeah, sure," she said and she kissed me on the lips. "I've some got good news though, before we talk about the couch."

"What?"

"Darin. You know how he hasn't been interested in anything, you know, besides video games and TV?"

"Yeah," but I wasn't really sure what she meant. Sadly, I had no idea what my kids liked or didn't like to do, except for TV. They were always watching TV.

"Well, I asked him about karate, if he thought he might like to try taking lessons. He's been getting picked on, I think."

"Really? Why do you say that?"

"Well, didn't you notice the scar on his cheek or the puffiness under his right eye?"

"No… I mean… Yeah."

And I had never really noticed my son before that very moment. He was short for his age, quiet, slightly overweight and pimply and Deidre had mentioned in the past that she thought it was sad that he didn't have any friends to speak of. No one ever came over to the house and he never seemed to get invited anywhere.

The same went for Sarah, though she was a little on the thin side. I noticed she wasn't girly at all, didn't like to have her nine-year-old hair brushed and didn't play with dolls or anything like that.

She just watched TV, her face nearly emotionless unless she was arguing with Darin about the television in the family room

"Well, there you go. I signed him up. I had to write a check because the karate school doesn't take credit cards."

"How much was the check for?"

And I was nervous. I thought I had all the checks in my possession but she must have gotten into one of the new checkbooks I kept in my desk drawer and I never did tell her that she couldn't write any checks.

Writing checks was just something Deidre didn't do.

"Well, I had to sign up for six months, so it was like almost nine hundred dollars"

My face froze. My sphincter actually contracted and I felt myself break out in some kind of sweat.

I didn't have nine hundred bucks in the checking account and I knew one bad check would send off a chain reaction of other bad checks as all the other checks I had written to pay off bills in the past couple of days would be on their way to being cleared.

And I was told by the bank to cut it out. Quit writing checks my account couldn't cash because they had been covering them for a while and slapping me with a twenty-five-dollar fee per check but they weren't going to do it anymore.

They were going to return the checks and not pay.

And then I would be screwed because I was falling behind again. The lease payments on both vehicles were sixty days past due and everything in the world was due on the fifteenth.

Gas, Electricity, Water, Telephone, Cellular Phone, Cable, Internet, American Express, Discover, Sears, all of them, due on the fifteenth.

Deidre wrote the check on the eleventh, which meant it had already hit the bank, more than likely, which meant my plan would unravel, which meant I had to kick in the last phase about three months earlier than I wanted to.

I took a deep breath and told Deidre that it was great what she did, signing Darin up for karate.

"He has to do something with his life," I said and there was just a little bit of guilt and sadness when I said that.

The collection calls came two nights later, on February 16th. I had been sleeping back in my bed again as Deidre had a sparkle in her eyes after I gave her that tennis bracelet.

Past due for this, past due for that left on the answering machine and Deidre looked at me pleadingly.

I showed her the palm of my hand to both quiet her and to tell her that I had everything under control.

"I'll call them back tomorrow from work," I told her.

"I want tonight to be... our night... A family night."

And she smiled sweetly at me and I told her I had one more thing for her and I dug in my pocket and fished out a small jewelry box.

"But Valentine's Day was two nights ago..."

"I want every day to be Valentine's Day."

And we went upstairs and I tore off my suit and threw it on the floor at the foot of the bed and we fucked like we were twenty-five again and I grabbed her ankles and pinned her legs behind her head.

She didn't bend like she did when she was twenty-five.

But she soldiered on and I came while staring at myself in the mirror over the vanity and I looked at everything except my pale stomach that shined through the dark like the underbelly of a fish swimming in a cold freshwater lake.

She smiled as I came and she grabbed my limp penis and put it in her mouth and my dick hadn't been in her mouth for at least thirteen years and she licked it tenderly and I became hard again as my middle-age went out the window.

We did it again. And this time it was the old standby doggy style and we both looked in the mirror and I felt born again.

We both came, loud and rejuvenated, and I could swear I saw our faces shine in the afterglow.

Or it could have been the light of the TV.

It was as if our relationship was entering a renaissance, as if we were back in the Eighties and money wasn't an issue and the whole world was ours to take.

As if the whole world was ours to buy.

But our renaissance was short lived.

It had to be short lived.

I wanted to finalize my plan right then after our session of nearly perfect sex. I felt good, energized, like I could kick the world's ass and it would be sweet revenge because the world had been kicking mine.

But I had to do one more house. I still had to set a pattern. I selected a random target and threw my old targets out the window.

It took two days.

I had to make sure there were no dogs or kids living in the next target.

I'm not afraid of guns or fire but strange dogs scare the crap out of me and it's probably because they always growl at me when I try to pet them.

So there you go...

The year is 2007, it's something like February 18th and I found a house in Birmingham with an Audi TT and a Lexus SUV in the driveway.

His and hers. How cute.

Their house was a new one, a McMansion, I think they're called. A towering house of glass and brick on a postage stamp sized lot surrounded by Colonial-type homes built probably in the Forties and Fifties.

The new house had no lawn, just building and driveway and it was hard to watch them without being obvious.

But I managed.

I waited until nightfall two nights in a row and I parked the Cadillac in the street and watched the house and they were a young professional couple, they didn't get home until after eight in the evening and they were the first victims that I actually got a good look at.

They were young, fit, attractive. He was tall, black or brown hair with clear skin. She was blonde, small-figured, pretty from my view from across the street.

It seemed like I picked a good easy target, no strings attached, just a young couple keeping to themselves in a big airy house.

I watched them unwind in front of the big picture window in the living room. They didn't bother to close the blinds as if they were deliberately displaying their looks and life to the otherwise darkened neighborhood.

I could see the wine glasses in their hands as they lounged in their living room with what seemed like every light in the house on. I watched them sitting there talking and smiling and laughing and they reminded me of Deidre and me back in our younger days, back when life was an easy pleasure.

At least that's the way I remember it.

I sat in my car and watched the couple live and both nights they went to bed at about eleven and I watched the lights in their oversized house turn off at once, like an eyelid closing shut, like a candle blown out by a sure and sharp breath.

I knew what I would do.

The third night, a Thursday, I told Deidre about another meeting, like I had the previous two nights.

"I'm trying to work my way out of debt," I told her. "I'm working in the corporate sales department now too, you know, moonlighting. This could be a huge commission check if I can get this company to get a few policies with us."

"But three nights in a row?"

"Well yeah, my contact there loves basketball. I gotta take him to the Pistons game, and this should do it. I should have 'im by then and then we can breathe easy… Daddy will buy Mommy a new pair of shoes."

Deidre smiled and kissed me on the cheek and gave my sweat suit a questioning look.

"You're going like that?"

"Yeah, the client wanted to make sure we went casual, you know, and my other play clothes don't fit anymore..." And that was true. Despite my recent penury I still managed to eat, and stress does hell on your metabolism and diet. My suits were barely fitting me and I had to pray each time I bent over at work because the buttons on my pants and shirts threatened to revolt and pop.

I drove and I parked a few blocks away, in back of an ornate Presbyterian church, sandwiching the Cadillac between the dumpster and low brick wall that separated the church from its affluent residential neighbors.

I walked.

I walked and you would be surprised how well lit the wealthy neighborhoods are. There are streetlights, porch lights, lights shining down from utility poles like spotlights.

In short, it was hard to walk in the shadows in Birmingham, so I didn't. I walked down the sidewalk casually and I was feeling casual, cool, calm, even though I was sweating like crazy and I had to take my gloves off and wipe my hands on my sweatpants because they were getting soaked.

I couldn't have the gun slip out of my hands.

I found my house.

And I said fuck under my breath.

I said fuck under my breath because the lights were still on and the pair were sitting on their couch drinking wine and laughing and she was wearing some kind of short silk bathrobe and he was wearing a tight plain white t-shirt and striped pajama pants and I said fuck again because the dude sure did have a lot of muscles.

I thought about aborting. I thought about going home and giving Deidre some more jewelry and trying to get lucky again and I don't mean just plain old missionary style lucky. I wanted to eat her out and then fuck her with my fist and then maybe try to fuck her in the ass and my cock started to rise as I stood in front of that house staring at the beautiful people drinking wine.

But I couldn't abort. Because if I aborted it would push me that much further back and my final battle would have to wait.

But the bills wouldn't wait and with my cock throbbing I thought about bankruptcy. I thought about getting a lawyer and laying my life in front of a court and asking for mercy.

But I couldn't do that. If I filed for bankruptcy the bosses at work would get wind of it and they had probably all heard about my episode with Reece at the Japanese restaurant and that was embarrassing enough.

No. I am a proud man. I'm a fighter, not a quitter, and bankruptcy would be quitting. It would be waving the white flag and telling the banks and credit card companies that they won.

I wasn't going to do that.

I moved to the back of the house and I thought about Deidre spread-eagle in our bed and I wished that I had bought her some lingerie, a garter belt and stockings, a leather corset, something raunchy. Maybe a belly chain.

But it was getting too late to decorate Deidre.

I went in the back of the house and they only had a swath of grass and a gigantic back deck and I was jealous of how little lawn mowing the muscle dude had to do in the summer and how if I had to do it all over I would have gotten the biggest house I could on the smallest lot because cutting grass can be a real bitch, especially when there's golf to play.

I walked up their massive deck and admired the stainless steel grill that glistened in the moonlight and it had a huge collection of knobs and burners and I figured this young couple had parties all summer long, their massive deck full of beautiful and smiling people and I was jealous because Deidre and I wanted to live the same kind of life and have beautiful friends to hang on our lives like so many human ornaments.

It didn't work out that way and I started to feel pity take over my heart and I thought about where my life went wrong. I thought about stopping and going back home and coming clean and telling Deidre *everything*, and I do mean everything, and maybe we could run away to some hick town in Kansas where no one gives a shit about possessions and the kids could thrive in clean air free of exhaust and competition.

But I said fuck all that. I pulled my ski mask over my face and I opened the sliding patio door open and to my surprise it was unlocked.

"Hello?" I yelled with my gun drawn as I wandered into the kitchen with granite topped counters and chrome appliances.

Muscle man came running into the kitchen and I shot him in the stomach and the chest and both knee caps but not the heart.

I didn't want to kill him, you see.

He fell on the hardwood floor that looked like it had just been mopped or never walked on and blood was gushing out and he moaned and cried as he clutched his stomach and I was impressed by the stopping power of my cheap back alley gun.

Because this guy fell hard and quick and he was a big son-of-a-bitch except he had a really narrow waist, as if his torso was some sort of fleshy, muscular V.

His little wife or girlfriend started screaming and I ran into the living room and grabbed her and she had a cell phone in her hand and she was trying to press buttons but her hands were shaking too much.

I didn't have to worry about a land line; they didn't have one.

I slapped the phone out of her hand and I stomped on it with my tennis shoe and that really didn't do anything but she didn't know that. I grabbed her quickly and hauled her into the kitchen.

I couldn't do anything with blinds wide open in the living room.

I pointed my gun at her and said, "Look at Little Dick here. (It was the meanest thing I could think of.) You wanna look like him?"

She was whimpering and crying and wailing just like they do in the movies, I shit you not.

She shook her head and said, "Please, I'll do anything!"

I smiled and I was still kind of hard, so I said, "Get on the table," and I was going to do it anyway after she was dead but I figured, what the hell, and I pulled her panties down and opened up her robe and she wasn't that great. She was too muscular. Her tits were firm and round but kind of small. I was surprised she didn't have implants.

Well, then again maybe she did. Her tits were small but my memory says they were perfect and firm, as if they were formed by some Italian sculptor during the Renaissance. Maybe she was just modest and didn't want big tits dragging her around.

Anyway, I did my thing. She screamed and cried and I pointed the gun at her and told her to shut up. Her big friend was dying on the floor and he couldn't move but he saw what I was doing and he said that I was a sick fuck.

I said you have no idea and I fired a shot into his shoulder as I came into his small tittied woman.

I said:

"Take that."

I pulled her off the table and told her to show me where her jewelry was and I tell you she had a shitload. She led me upstairs to her bedroom and I would have to guess their bedroom took up like the whole upstairs. It was huge. She had pearls and diamonds all over her bedroom and I stuffed my pockets and I saw Muscleman's wallet on the nightstand and I opened it up because I wanted his cash but he only had a twenty dollar bill and a bunch of credit cards.

"It fucking figures," I said and I told the lady to get on her bed and lie face down.

She did.

I shot her in the back of the head just once and she stopped shaking and whimpering instantly.

I got the starter fluid and poured it all over her bed and lit it.

I walked back to the church under all the lights and the sirens were sounding by the time I got to my car.

The Birmingham hit made the news.

Of course it did.

The media said the crime was vicious and they assumed correctly that I was responsible for other heinous crimes in the area.

I knew that a neighbor would see the flames and smoke from the upstairs and call 911. I knew the Birmingham Fire Department would appear full force with ambulances at the ready and I knew Muscleman would survive.

Which he did.

He was listed in critical condition and the media said I was a monster. The media said I was dangerous and I may or may not be acting alone and that robbery appears to be my only motive though I don't take much.

I thought about writing a letter to the *Detroit Free Press* with some sort of manifesto but I chose not to.

A good soldier doesn't let his enemy know what he's up to. Guerillas strike when the strikes aren't expected.

Take September 11, 2001. Say what you will but it was a brilliant tactical move against the "enemy" by the terrorists. It brought our country to its emotional knees and it scared the crap out of us.

Fear is a powerful weapon.

And people in metropolitan Detroit were starting to get a little afraid of me and I've never intimidated anyone in my life. Far from it. I was picked on in junior high because I was small and had bad skin. That and I was a know-it-all little shit, but that has nothing to do with the now and my War.

So why did I let Muscleman live?

Because I had to establish a slightly skewed pattern. I had to let a victim survive so it wouldn't seem so odd the next time around.

March 4th, 2007. A pivotal day in my life and I let some time elapse since the Birmingham hit and I have to admit I was a little paranoid. I was always looking over my shoulder while walking the hallways of Midwestern. I was always glancing in my rearview mirror and looking out the window while at home to make sure no one was following or casing me.

Someone like the police.

But there was no one. Only bill collectors and harassing messages on my answering machine.

Pay or else.

And I did get a notice of foreclosure in the mail and I was fine with that. I yawned when I opened up the letter and I didn't answer it because I knew I would soon make everything right.

Deidre wasn't so calm. Her van got repossessed just the day before and it was really bad because it was while she was at the junior high school talking to the principal about the circle of bullies who had been terrorizing Darin at lunchtime.

The karate hadn't paid off yet even though the check had cleared.

Deidre decided to show up just before the end of the school day. She got to talk to the principal and she got nothing from him except that same old song and dance that principals always give to complaining parents.

"We'll look into it, Ms. Dash," he probably said as he had his hand on the back of her shoulder, gently guiding her out of his office.

Apparently, the repo man followed Deidre from the house and he was hooking up her van just as all the kids were walking out of the school. A lot of them were being picked up by their own mothers, who also happened to know Deidre and saw her running down the street past the idling minivans and school buses as her van was being towed away.

She told me about this in a strained and tearful voice that was barely above a whisper when I got home that night. She told me she tried to call the police from her cell phone but it wasn't working for some reason.

It got shut off, I told her, my voice as flat as a stagnant pond on a windless day.

"Well that's just great... That's just fucking great," she told me and if she didn't look and sound so defeated she would have thrown something at me.

But she was down for the count and I could see the life had been taken out of her heart and face. She was pale and her eyes were dim even though they were wide open.

She started crying and went upstairs to the bedroom and called her mother. And I know that her mother said I told you so, and why don't you come back home? And Deidre probably said something like no, Chas will figure this out, he always does, he makes good money, we just got ahead of ourselves...

I sat in the great room with Darin and Sarah as they watched TV.

Darin got up and left and went to his room as soon as I sat down. He didn't talk to me at all after the van got repossessed because I knew he was embarrassed and I figured it didn't matter by that point.

March 4th was as good a day as any to finalize my plan.

It was simple, really. It took a whole lot less effort than my other hits.

And absolutely no heart.

I waited until the kids were asleep and Deidre took a while. I was lying in the bed next to her, listening to her sob gently and I told her everything was going to be okay. The big corporate sale went through and that meant a twenty-grand commission check for me by the end of the month and then I would *buy* her a minivan or anything she wanted.

"You know, a good used vehicle," I said and I stroked the back of her head because she had her back turned toward me. I promised to get her a new cell phone, one of those Bluetooth things that attached to the ear and that perked her up a little bit, probably because all the other women in the neighborhood had them attached to their skulls.

"That'd be nice," she said and the sobbing started to subside and it went away completely when I said, "I'm sorry.

"I'm sorry for everything, and for whatever else you want to blame me for, but trust me, all of our troubles are going to be over soon. I can absolutely promise you that." And I kissed her on the back of the neck and I felt my cock start to swell and this was going to be the hard part. I toyed with the idea of forcing myself on her because I knew she wasn't in the mood for sex.

But this was going to be my last chance.

I grabbed the hem of her nightgown and started to pull it up.

And then I stopped. I decided to let her sleep because sooner would be better.

She fell asleep and I knew that because I could hear her quietly snore and gently grind her teeth, something she always did in her sleep when she was feeling stressed out.

"You don't know stress," I said as I got out of bed at about one in the morning. I reached under my nightstand and pulled on some surgical gloves that I bought for this final piece of my plan and grabbed the gun from under the mattress.

I stood at the foot of the bed and fired. Three shots, all in the head.

She never woke up, and I could hear the blood pour out of her like water out of a running faucet.

I'm sure the kids woke up.

I ran into their bedrooms and I shot them too and I might have cried a little bit but the life I gave them really wasn't worth living.

I went into the kitchen and stepped out on the patio. I broke the patio door with a decorative rock from the yard and kicked the shards of glass into the kitchen and stepped through it, so very careful as to not get a stitch of my clothes stuck in the jagged glass left in the door.

I turned around and locked the door.

I went back upstairs, took some of Deidre's jewelry out of her jewelry boxes and tipped them over. I started pulling stuff out of all of our drawers and basically ransacked the bedroom. I then poured lighter fluid on the bed and lit it on fire.

I had to move quickly.

I went to the top of the stairs and fired the gun in my thigh.

A bullet feels like a hot knife with serrated blades that are twisted once they get inside you.

I knew that wouldn't be sufficient.

I fired, aiming the gun right at my appendix.

Or where I thought my appendix might be.

I remember a flash of powder and pain and blood oozing out of my body.

I tried to walk down the stairs but I slid and fell and I left a trail of blood behind me.

But still, though I barely remember doing this, I opened the side door going into the garage very carefully. I threw the gun, gloves and jewelry toward the ceiling so it would fall behind the drywall that was never properly insulated because I had hired a shabby and fly-by-night contractor to finish and paint the garage. I did this very carefully and precisely because I could barely stand and to make things look genuine I walked to the Cadillac and tried to open the door, making sure I got my bloody handprint on the handle.

The Cadillac was locked of course so I walked back to the house. I went back inside and I thought about calling 911 but I couldn't make it past the washer and dryer.

I curled up in a fetal position and fell asleep and I remember smoke from the upstairs drifting down and wrapping itself around me in a warm, warm fog.

I woke up several hours later and I couldn't move. I heard the blip of hospital machines and I was attached to several and I couldn't tell you what they were all for. It took me more than a moment to remember everything, to remember fire and smoke and blood and debt.

It took me more than a moment to remember I was in the middle of my own private war.

It took even longer to remember that war is hell.

I opened my eyes and the room was bright, well lit and the sun was pouring through an open window and I remember the light hurt my eyes.

I tried to turn my head but I couldn't. The feeling returned to my body but my limbs felt numb or barely there and I felt like I was wrapped tight in sheets or maybe some sort of shroud.

Really, I wasn't sure if I was alive.

My mind focused after a moment and I stared at the things above me, fluorescent lighting and ceiling tiles, vents, fire sprinklers.

A voice said, "He's awake."

And then there was a rustling of chairs and feet and more voices singing a chorus that sounded like it was coming at me from the bottom of some deep and empty well.

Mr. Dash? Charles? Chuck? Chip?

Chas?

I tried to open my mouth. I tried to say something stupid. Something like, where am I? Something like, where's the gun?

But no, my mouth wouldn't move and all anyone heard was mmmmphf, or something like that.

And it was a good thing that my mouth didn't move at that point because things started coming to me in quick flashes of memory. Flashes of bullets and fire. Flashes of blood and death.

Of creation and destruction. Of my plan.

Of the death of my family by my own hand.

I knew I had an audience, so I said what I thought they needed to hear.

I could feel the words travel from my brain to my stomach and then up my spine to my tongue and lips and I could feel my tongue move slow and thick behind my teeth as if it was a large grizzly bear ending its hibernation. I felt my mouth open and my lips part like a crack in the bottom of a dry riverbed.

"Deidre?" I gasped and think Sylvester Stallone in the first Rocky movie after getting his ass beat by Carl Weathers. Think of his face all bloody and beaten and the pure enduring love from his voice as he said, "Adrian!"

A scurry of feet and faces peering above me and some of the faces I recognized.

My mother, my older brother and maybe the ghost of my still living father above them looking proud of me but also shaking his head.

And there were other faces. Official looking faces. Stern faces that looked like they wanted to carve me up and flay me open.

"Deidre?" I mouthed again to those official looking faces.

"Take it easy, Chip." My brother laid his hand gently on my shoulder and it was the first time he touched me since we were kids, since he bloodied my nose when I was in junior high when I stole his collection of *Hustler* magazines and my brother had gotten old since the last time I looked closely at his face, and that may have been since childhood too. He lived just fifteen minutes from me but I never noticed the disappearing hair or the wrinkles in his forehead and around his mouth and the pale skin under his eyes was as dark as the night sky surrounding the moon.

He looked like shit. He looked like life had beaten him up even though he was pulling down six figures and had a hot enough wife.

He looked like me before I started my war and I thought about asking him if he wanted to fight, later, after I got better.

But I didn't ask him anything.

"Deidre?" I gasped again, but this time a little louder.

"Charlie, honey," my mother said with her withered face and thin, thin lipsticked lips. "I am so sorry."

"Not now," an official female face said. "Don't tell him now. Wait. Wait till he comes around a little more. Wait for his heart and blood to stabilize. He won't understand right now and if he does it would be a shock to his system..."

I understood just fine.

"Deidre!" I yelled and I raised my head up as if I was going to try to get out of bed but so many hands gently pushed me back in place.

"Mr. Dash," another official face, this time male and tense, "can you talk?"

"Not yet," said the official female face and she had to be a doctor or nurse. Her cheeks were smooth and warm and her eyes looked tired but considerate. "Maybe tomorrow. We will call you, Detective, just as soon as he is stable and knows what happened."

The detective stormed off. I could hear his heels on the linoleum.

My father disappeared, too. I saw him fade into the fluorescence above my head, just like the ghost he had always been.

March 11th. The day I woke up.

I shouted Deidre's name for an hour and then someone put something in my IV and the room grew dark.

I woke up, again, and it must have been evening as there was only artificial light in the room. I was aware of my surroundings instantly but I didn't know how long I'd been there. I didn't know how I lost consciousness or what happened to my house or if the police or anyone else had figured out what I was up to.

I could move my head this time, though it was uncomfortable. I expected an audience to be waiting at my bedside.

But there was no one. I thought I was completely alone until my eyes adjusted some more and I saw my brother sitting in a chair along the side of my bed, his head tilted toward the TV watching a rerun of *Law and Order*.

He turned toward me after a moment, as if he could tell I was staring at him.

"Hey," he said softly, out-of-character, and I saw a trace of sadness in his eyes and his eyes had never been sad before, not even when our dog got hit by a car when we were in first and second grade and the dog was not quite a year old, a black lab that we called Shadow and it followed Jeff and me around all the time and we loved it a lot.

Our father had promised to get us another dog but the other dog never did make it into our family.

"You all right?" he asked even though I obviously wasn't all right and I was wondering why it was Jeff that was there with me, sitting by himself in the almost-dark.

It was because my brother was the one that was designated to fill me in. He was the one to tell me what happened with my life.

There was no one else who wanted to do it. No one else felt close enough to me to tell me my own family had been killed and burned.

"You've been out for a week, bud," he said.

I looked at him.

"You've got burns on thirty percent of your body."

I gave him another look and then I became aware of the burns. The right side of my face and chest felt tender and crisp and tight, as if moving my muscles would break the skin.

"See…" and he shifted in his chair. "There's been this arson burglar rapist going around. Killing people and taking jewelry and stuff and, well… you were one of his victims. You and Deidre and the kids."

I thought about what I had to say. I hoped the gun remained behind the garage wall and undiscovered and I feared the police going over my house with a fine tooth comb looking for evidence like they do on television.

I started to panic and sweat a little and maybe even tremble, I think, because Jeff scooted his chair closer to the bed and rested his hand on my arm.

"Take it easy," he said with a tenderness I'd never seen from him or anyone else in my family before, including my mother.

"Where are they?" I rasped and I squeezed my eyes shut for effect but the right side of my face hurt like hell when I did that as the muscles in my cheek were forced to move.

He took a deep breath and turned his gaze to the floor.

"You were the only survivor."

I opened my eyes and looked at him. I didn't say anything. I didn't know what to say and I think I might have cried a little bit though my face and body felt too dry to generate tears.

"What do you mean?" I asked and I know my voice was perfectly rasped and choked.

I knew damn well what he meant.

"Deidre and the kids... They..." and his voice trailed off and he started to cry and I'll be damned if I ever saw Jeff cry except for that last time our father laid a belt to him when he was about eleven or twelve and got caught beating off to our mother's Sears catalog.

"What are you saying?"

"They're gone, Chip. Gone. All gone. They're in heaven now."

I was silent.

"See, this guy, this sick, sick fuck did this. He... he gets off on robbing and burning or something and I guess the police have some leads. They brought some preacher in for questioning the other day but they had to let him go, not enough evidence or something."

I perked up when he said that.

"Preacher?"

"Yeah, I guess this preacher said people victimized, people like you, were getting the wrath of god for a wayward life or some shit. I guess he said it at his church, in front of everybody, like he was glad of it or something, and somebody in his congregation mentioned it to the cops. They've been looking at him. Hell, the news people have been looking at him, but there's nothing. Not yet. But we're going to nail that bastard, I tell you, 'cause I think he's the one."

I felt a lot better after that.

"So, Deidre... and Darin... and Sarah... gone?"

My brother nodded, his middle-aged skin staring at the linoleum floor.

"Yep. No pain, either. The bastard shot them before..."

And he explained as delicately as he could about the fire and how my house was a disaster but Midwestern had already inspected the damage and had checks cut to fix everything.

"I hired the contractors," he explained. "I hope you don't mind..."

I shook my head even though it hurt to do so and that was even better news.

The police were obviously done combing the place over.

"Thank god you have good insurance, but then I guess you would, seeing how you're in the business."

And I thought, exactly.

You are exactly right.

But I didn't say anything.

I just let my brother go. I let him talk and I didn't interrupt and I was growing tired.

A nurse came and said something cross to my brother about not letting anyone know I was awake and some kind of school-age doctor followed the nurse as if he was trying to smell her ass and they both asked me how I was doing and there were readings and charts and adjustments made on the IV drips and I felt my mind grow heavy as I heard my brother say, "I was just letting him know what's happened to the rest of his life."

And then I fell into the sweetest and deepest sleep I have ever known.

I knew right then, as I drifted away on waves of deadened pain, what it felt like to sleep like a free, free man.

I was in the hospital for three weeks. I missed the funerals. I missed the holes in the ground and the sparse crowd of mourners. I missed the stories in the newspapers, but I did get to see them on TV.

There really is no difference.

I wasn't lonely for those three weeks. I slept and recovered and I had to entertain a parade of normally indifferent relatives and co-workers who offered their condolences and support.

My father was still a ghost.

I was ready to scream each time someone asked, "Is there anything I can do?"

The police came, too. Several times. Fat suburban middle-aged plain-clothes types who really didn't seem to give a shit about anything except for punching that retirement clock and I can't say I would be any different. I can't say I would give a shit about a guy like me in a hospital bed. I was wary of them at first.

I thought they might be on to me and it isn't like I'm an expert arsonist or anything. I probably left a well-lit trail of evidence leading right to me if they looked hard enough.

No, I'm no expert thief or rapist or murderer.

I'm a zealot. A revolutionary. A survivor.

The police prodded me a little bit, gently, just to see if I had something to hide, but they didn't push me too hard. They didn't want to give a guy who had burns all over his body and a dead family too rough of a time.

It was obvious they didn't want to work too hard. They didn't want to have to sweat interviewing me.

"Why would someone do this to you?" a fat mustachioed cop in a good suit asked me.

"I have no idea," I said. What else was I supposed to say?

"No enemies, no jealous friends or co-workers?"

"No, no, and no." And I wanted to tell him that I really didn't have any friends and co-workers typically hated me.

"You know," I said, just to throw something out there, "I'm the vice-president of claim processing. Some customers that have been denied claims in the past might have been angry with me. Was that preacher fellow a customer of Midwestern?"

The cop shrugged and his partner, a middle-aged woman in worn nylons and a tight skirt that wasn't supposed to be that way said that there was definitely a connection to Midwestern Accident and Life.

"We just don't know what is, at least not yet."

And that was it.

I finally went home and the work on the house was mostly done except for the portable dumpster still sitting in my front yard that the contractors used to throw all the burnt parts of my house and memories into. I stayed home for a few weeks after that, making the most of my newfound freedom and my wealth.

That's right.

Wealth.

I became wealthy.

Not Bill Gates wealthy. Not wealthy enough to retire.

But remember, I'm in the insurance business. I shopped the competition years ago.

I had policies. Policies on Deidre. Policies on Sarah and Darin.

Midwestern had to pay me. Five hundred thousand on Deidre. A hundred thousand on each of the kids and a hundred and fifty thousand for my misfortunate accident that left me disfigured. I had a few policies elsewhere, with other companies, you know, the good and big ones. Companies that weren't shady like my company.

Companies like State Farm, Allstate, you name it. I had little policies with each of them.

And I knew the loopholes. I knew some would try to find a way not to pay me, even Midwestern. Especially Midwestern.

But I had death by fire coverage. I had death by bullets coverage. I had vicious crime coverage. I had death and dismemberment. I had oodles of supplemental insurance and lost wages coverage.

I had insurance on Deidre's potential future earnings.

I had it all covered.

I didn't leave a stone unturned.

Now, I didn't phone all of my policies in at once. I didn't want to seem greedy. I didn't want to bring too much suspicion on myself.

And my work made it easy.

Our CEO, some young dink who started after me but he had all the credentials and charisma in the world, phoned me at the hospital.

The checks are being cut, he said, he just asked if some of the payments could be deferred.

"We don't usually have to pay all at once like that, you know."

I knew only all too well.

"That's fine," I said into the phone that was held to my ear by a nurse as it was early in my hospital stay. "Bless you, sir," I said, just like a character from a Dickens novel. I wanted it to seem like I really didn't need the money, even though the police could have figured out that I really did if they looked at me at all.

I went home.

The fire damage had been fixed and most of the burned items were thrown away, things like me and Deidre's bed. I knew I'd have to order a new one. The blood from Darin's and Sarah's bedrooms was mostly gone and their rooms had been straightened up by someone, more than likely Jeff's wife, who I always wanted to do.

I closed the door to the kids' rooms and I've barely opened them again.

Eventually, though, the money came in and bills got paid off. Accounts closed. Mortgages paid and I went back to work. My disfigurement has no bearing on my work at Midwestern. In fact, it's an asset. Absolutely no one will fuck with me. I have become the CEO's right hand man as of late. My salary is now $250,000 and I don't have a financial care in the world.

So you would think I stopped fighting the war then, wouldn't you?

You would be wrong.

But let's get go back to before I became the CEO's right hand man. Let's go back to those days just after I got out of the hospital.

I took three weeks off of work and I kind of refocused during that time and no one gave me any shit.

I had to adjust to a couple of things, mainly widowerhood and disfigurement.

That and I hit three more houses, in a similar fashion, but there were no survivors.

Nor will there ever be a survivor again.

That's because a survivor can still pay off his debt and I want all those debts to go unpaid.

Being a widower was the easy part and is still the easy part. I come and go as I please, I watch whatever I want on TV, and the inside of the house is pretty much trashed, though I do my best to keep appearances up on the outside.

But I can pay someone to take care of the outside and I suppose I could pay someone to take care of the inside, you know, hire a cleaning lady three days a week and I can afford it but I really don't want anyone to take a look on the inside. I don't want anyone to see the porno movies and stained sheets. At least not yet. I am lonesome, sometimes. I feel guilty.

Sometimes.

And sometimes I miss the kids and Deidre, especially Deidre, but I have to be honest, I miss her vagina more than I miss her. Even though I barely saw her vagina in the last couple of years, I am still full of so many torrid memories of music and mirrors and lingerie.

War. War is hell and I haven't handled the disfigurement nearly as well as being a widower.

The doctors did a good job on me. The hospital was nice and clean and probably pretty damn expensive.

Thank god for health insurance.

But there is only so much a doctor or science can do. A doctor can graft skin but it's not the same skin that you had before some tragedy.

So what do I look like?

Well, it's healed some now, but after it happened, it looked like the right side of my face was a marshmallow roasted way too long.

Now, it looks somewhat normal, like as if someone put a branding iron on my cheek and held it there just long enough to make my flesh sizzle and my right eye really isn't quite right because the skin around it isn't as fleshy as it is on the left side of my face and there is a discomfort there, always a bit of pain as the nerve endings are not as insulated as well as they used to be so sleep is tough, especially when I roll over at night and accidentally wind up laying on my right side.

There is a bag under my left eye, a dark circle like a bruise and if the pain doesn't keep me awake then the War does.

There is always plotting and strategizing that keeps me awake. There are always ideas about how to throw the enemy off guard and I am pissed at the enemy, especially when I look in the mirror, because my disfigurement is their fault, if you get right down to it.

So, I get stared at. Girls at the office won't go out with me so I'm back to hookers because they have to go out with me if they want to get paid.

But I'm not here to tell you about hookers.

I'm here to tell you about my life, about how and why I've gotten to where I am and I'd have to say I still feel pretty good about my life. I took a meaningless existence and gave it meaning and you can't get meaning without sacrifice.

I sacrificed my family and my face.

Anyway, I went back to work and I rose through the ranks once more and I was surprised how much they wanted to pay me because I didn't think the guys on the top floor really got paid any more than I did.

But I was wrong.

I've become something like the CEO's special ops kind of guy. I fire and scold. I motivate lackluster managers. I deal with our independent agents who can't sell shit and I tell them they have to sell or lose our tag. You know the independent agent, the guy selling insurance in some crappy office in a strip mall; he's usually a little overweight and wears a bad suit that used to fit better about three thousand donuts ago.

Guys like my father. Old men wearing diamond rings on their pinkies and their wives wear fur coats and they go to steakhouses on the weekends and declare how damn good they are and how sweet life is.

They find meaning in cuts of beef.

Six months after I got out of the hospital, Midwestern gave me another hundred grand and I became debt-free except for my mortgage and I had no problem making that payment as it's only me to feed and clothe.

I wanted to get a new car but my credit rating still sucked even though I had some money and that got me a little angry so I drove around all day until I found a house with two Cadillacs in the driveway and I did them in two nights later, an old couple, probably not a lot of debt, but oh well.

The only hardship I've really encountered in the last year is fighting the war. It got a little more challenging finding targets in metro Detroit. I mean, I couldn't just keep on using the Midwestern high-risk client list, someone eventually would have gotten wise someday and start warning every Midwestern consumer.

So I went to meetings. Alcoholics Anonymous, Gamblers Anonymous, you know, meetings in community centers and church basements. Meetings for support groups, drug and sexual addicts, children of abusive parents, you name it.

Debtors Anonymous.

Someone who has drunk or gambled their life away usually owes someone a lot of money and they bleed the details of their personal lives in front of these support groups and that's where I find my targets now, except I've had to spread out of the Detroit area a little bit. I'll spend a weekend in Cincinnati or Kalamazoo, Grand Rapids or Fort Wayne.

It doesn't matter, there's debt and misery, and for your sake, keep your financial house in order.

You just might smell blood and smoke if you don't.

This is today. Now. You could maybe call this an epilogue if this was a real story. You could call this the afterword or maybe the final chapter but it doesn't matter what you want to call it because it's the end and maybe the end of the war. Maybe I wasn't honest with you or myself. Maybe I'm not as clever as I thought I was.

Maybe I'm a bad soldier who had a hot streak.

Let's go back a couple of days. A Monday afternoon in 2009 and I decided to drive over to my father's office and I don't know what made me do that. Maybe it was because he all but disowned me after Deidre and the kids died. My brother said he was like that with everyone, even our mother, and how they've become more like two roommates sharing a house rather than husband and wife. I don't know. The least he could have done was see me while I was in the hospital and say he was sorry about the passing of his grandchildren and daughter-in-law. That would have been the decent thing to do, even if I was the responsible party.

I drove to his office, not far from my office, and I didn't realize it had been a decade since I last stepped into the place, a little stand-alone building along Eleven Mile Road in Warren. The neighborhood had gone from ashes to prosperity back to ashes again.

I entered his office and there were no customers, his Lincoln sitting in the cracked asphalt parking lot like a homely and overdressed girl at a school dance without a single boy asking her to dance. The place was unchanged largely, the same fake wood paneled walls and low carpet and it resembled a vanity-laden time capsule with all the plaques on the wall, Independent Agent of the Year for 1967, 1969, 1972, '73, '74, '75, '77, '78, '79 and 1981. And the plaques were mixed with photographs of old golf outings with his now dead buddies and customers, even a few local celebrities from the 1970s, Detroit radio and television personalities who bought insurance from my father and I could tell you there is absolutely no way in hell a celebrity would walk into his office now. He was sitting at his desk, which sat underneath the picture window that seemed so much dirtier than I remembered it. He was wearing a decent enough gray suit but the tie was ugly, something red yellow and blue and he was breathing hard into his oxygen tank and his eyes flashed with recognition and horror when he saw it was me.

He hadn't seen my new face before, but I know he was told.

"Hello," I said and I grabbed a cup of coffee from his ancient Mr. Coffee coffeemaker.

He grunted, a wheeze and a snort and he touched the plastic tubes going into his nose.

"I was driving by," I said. "I thought I'd stop by and say hello. You know, it's been a while."

"Not long enough," he said, and that surprised me. My father was never proud of my brother and me; he was always proudest of himself.

But I never thought he hated me, and that's why his behavior since Deidre and the kids passed was so puzzling to me.

Why did I wait so long before confronting him? I don't know, pride maybe, that and I was and am a bit preoccupied. I would think about him during odd moments of melancholy, lamenting the misery of my childhood and the destruction of my family and then my thoughts would shift—to fire and war, beer and pornography, money and golf.

"What did I do to piss you off so much?" and I was never so candid with my father. Since high school, our conversations were about money and business and life goals and plans and they were never ever more than skin deep. We never discussed family or the past, we just talked about retirement planning and the future, our lives plodding along like empty freight trains.

"Everything, you did everything. You know what you did. What you've done." And he reached into his desk and grabbed a pack of Pall Malls and lit one with his shaking hand.

And I'd never seen his hands shake before. He suddenly seemed so very mortal and pathetic to me.

"What do you mean?"

"You killed your wife and kids and a lot of other people, that's what you did."

His words didn't surprise me or stun me and I think he recognized that by my reaction or lack of a reaction. No indignation. No denial. Nothing except a slow slow nod and then I said:

"How did you know?"

"Just did. Maybe a father knows. Maybe it's something I would have done, might have done, but you're a goddamn idiot, that's what you are, and I know you, deep down I know you, and maybe you're a little too much like me, maybe you do all you can to keep things going," and this he said with a wave of his arms to indicate his sorry little office and oxygen tank, as if the tank was just there to let him keep breathing in the past. I don't know, but I knew what I had to do.

No one could or can know what I'm up to.

I walked up to him, yanked the tubes out of his nose and grabbed the large ceramic ashtray and smashed the top of his liver spotted head, a burst of dead Pall Malls dancing in the air and landing like ash on his head and suit. He crashed into his desk face first and he was out but still breathing.

I went out to my car and grabbed some of my things. Lighter fluid and matches. I went back inside and lit the wastebasket next to his desk on fire and then I doused him and the floor of his office in fluid.

I walked out and drove away and my heart was racing faster than it ever had. I smacked myself in the head. I should have made it look like a robbery at the very least, and that's where I fucked up.

How do I know I fucked up?

Because it's been two days now and all day and every day a squad car is in the parking lot at work, just cruising around with the driver staring at the top of the Midwestern Pyramid. Each night and all night a police cruiser rolls past my house and I know it's only a matter of time before the knock comes on my door.

I am getting ready to go now. My father's funeral. The family is ignorant and blissful and my father didn't have an empty will. There is an inheritance, a lot for my brother and even more for my mother and not enough for me.

So I guess I'll have to take that.

ABOUT THE AUTHOR

David LaBounty lives in suburban Detroit with his wife and two sons. His poetry and prose has appeared in several print and online journals. He has served in the Navy and has held jobs as a member of the blast team in a gold mine in northern Nevada, as a mechanic, a reporter and as a salesman. He is the author of *The Perfect Revolution* and *The Trinity*, published by Silverthought Press in 2006 and 2007.